THE *Winter* EXPERIENCE

The Seasons Experience Collection
Book One

Eli Summers

I wanted to think of something funny, but that didn't seem very professional, so I'll just thank my grandmother Glenda Bettin.

I also need to thank those that contributed to my GoFundMe to get this book printed and sent out;

Shauna Martens
Dean Afseth
Jaret Martens
KC
Glenda & Chris Domitrovich
Linda & Alvin Thompson
Juanita Schwebius
Jaimie Horn

Thank you.

Copyright © 2014 by Eli Summers
All rights reserved. This book or any portion thereof
may not be reproduced or used in any manner whatsoever
without the express written permission of the publisher
except for the use of brief quotations in a book review.

This is a work of fiction. Any resemblance to real people,
Locations or settings is purely coincidental.

Praise for *The Winter Experience*

"Some stories will take you on a journey, sometimes an unexpected ride. Those stories will make you feel and live this journey. I think this is one of those stories." – *Simaagn*

"From the first moment they meet, this delightfully innocent story of young love captures your heart and takes you on an emotional journey that will make you laugh, make you cry, make you smile, make you appreciate all the moments, both special and every day, it takes to build a relationship as truly beautiful as Mattie and Morgan's. These characters cling to your heart long after you've turned the last page!" – *Eryn Summers*

"Eli plays with your heart from beginning to end. You'll squeal, laugh, cry, and everything in between." – *RT Cipher*

"In my eyes [The Winter Experience] ranks as one of the greatest books I will ever have the pleasure of reading. The characters come alive and they make you both laugh and cry. I rarely ever cry while reading and this one made me cry."

"It is a beautiful love story. I don't think anyone else could have told Mattie and Morgan's story better." – *Gingerdream*

"The moment I started reading, I couldn't put it away anymore. Every character in this book is written with love and Mattie and Morgan are an incredibly sweet couple." – *Catherine Micqu*

The Winter Experience

Prologue

I looked down at the photographs pinned throughout the scrapbook. I ran my fingers throughout the pages, remembering everything about the boy in the pictures. I never thought in a million years Morgan Winters and I would have ever started something as exciting as we did. From the tennis practices to the video game sessions in our underwear, I was in love with every part of his life. I loved every minute I spent with him, and I never wanted to leave his side no matter what.

I looked down to see the first picture we ever took together... it was the first day of high school. Everyone was nervous to meet new people, start at a new school, and get new teachers, but Morgan seemed cool and collected with his camera in hand and a smile on his face. He had no worries. He wasn't interested in the future. He was only interested in what was happening right now, in the present.

It was a cool September day, and summer had left us

behind as fall moved in quickly. It had gone from the blistering heat of the summer sun to the cool air of fall. I had a sweater hugged tightly to my body, and my fingers were getting slightly cold as I walked through the courtyard to the main doors. I looked up at the seven story building, not knowing how the hell this was a school and not an apartment block. I turned around to say goodbye to the open air of the world and say hello to the cramped hallways of Levitt High School. Sighing, I turned on my heels and went to open the door, only to touch the hand of someone beside me.

I quickly pulled away and turned to who the hand belonged to, and my heart stopped right there. I could feel my breath hitch, and my lungs wanted to burst. The boy standing beside me was gorgeous, well at least gorgeous in my eyes. His mousy brown hair clung tightly to the sides of his face, and he was wearing some ripped up skinny jeans and a red band tee-shirt. A small hoodie clung to his figure as headphones bounced with his movements. I found myself staring at this boy as a small smile danced across the thin lips of his face.

"S-sorry. I'm n-new here." I cursed at myself for stuttering. That's not how I normally talk, but I found it hard to find words with this boy staring at me. I quickly moved backwards, letting him open the door, but he just stood there and stared at me, that beautiful smile never leaving his face.

"It's all good. So you're in grade 10 are you? I'm in grade 12, so this will be my last year at Levitt." The way he talked seemed so effortless like he wasn't scared of anything. I was jealous. I wanted to be as carefree as that, but here I was, staring at this boy and trying to think of something cool to say.

"Oh. Out with the old and in with the new." I caught myself, and red started to form on my cheeks as his smile started to grow. "I mean, not that you're old. You're only in grade 12, but you know... I'm new to this school, and you're about to leave and that I guess makes you old. Not old as in grandpa old, because why would you be in school if you were as old as a grandpa? Why would you even be alive, y'know? Not saying nobody's grandpa is alive..." I was rambling, and I really hated when this started happening. God dammit I probably sounded like an idiot.

"You're cute, did you know that? Here, I'm on the yearbook committee, let's get a picture of the new and the old, shall we?"

Without any further words, he wrapped his arm around my shoulders and put the camera in front of our faces. He quickly snapped a picture before I even had time to fix my hair. I stood there with a dumbfounded look on my face, trying to think of what to say next, "Do I get a copy of that?"

The smirk returned to his lips, "What are you going to do with it? Masturbate to my beautiful face?"

I was now all shades of red, trying my best to not giggle or something really stupid. I looked up at him, and I saw his eyes, they were dancing and glistening with amusement. I wanted so badly to look into his eyes as I kissed his lips and put my hand through his hair. It was at that moment, I think I fell in love with Morgan Winters. I think it was that moment that I wanted nothing more than to be with him every day of my life, until the end of my life.

"Hey, Morgan, who's the new kid?" I heard a boisterous and deep voice call from behind us, and I turned to see another boy jogging to us. I turned back to Morgan, who was not going to be taken away from me by one of his friends. What if I never got to see him ever again? Well, of course, I would see him, because we go to the same school, but would this be the last time I was ever able to talk to him? I didn't think I would ever get this close to him again.

"I never did get your name, kid. I'm Morgan Winters. You are?"

I thought for a second, trying to think of a cool name, but decided on my own, "Mattie."

"Well, I'll see you later, Mattie."

He walked into the school, and I suddenly realized I never answered him. I swung open the door and yelled inside, "I'll only do that if you want me to, Morgan." I saw him turn around, the same devilish smirk on his face."I'll have one by the end of the day for you. Maybe I'll have to print an extra copy for you."

Chapter One

As I sifted through the box of old photos, I quickly noticed all the pictures of nature and bugs. Morgan was a free spirit, and he loved to take pictures of anything and everything he could see. He believed that everyone forgot the little things in life, and he always wanted to remind people of these things. He would take pictures of absolutely everything, down to the smallest moments of life. He always had his camera slung around his neck, and his memory card bursting with pictures.

I found the first picture he ever took of me and his little sister, Jenny. We were in the same math and science classes, and we soon made a bond I will never forget. I had come from a small school where I was not the most popular kid, but she took me under her wing and soon we were best friends. This was one of the good moments he caught, one of my favourite memories. He took it during lunch, when she dragged me to sit with her.

I was looking at the sheet of paper in my hand, which was difficult considering the shaking from my nervousness overtook me at points. Room 313 was written in bold letters next to the teacher's name and the class she was teaching. I looked at the door and noticed the numbers, this was where I needed to be.

I walked inside, putting the paper safely in my back pocket. I noticed everyone sitting down, talking to people they had met, the friends they had gained. I found an open seat and turned to a boy talking about football. "Is this seat taken by anyone?"

He gave me a stink eye because, apparently, I had interrupted a very important conversation. "No," he spat at me and then turned back to his friend, the Saskatchewan Roughriders coming into the conversation. I held my breath but took a seat, before noticing the girl beside me engulfed in a book. I read the cover and immediately felt happy, she was reading something by David Levithan, one of my favourite authors.

"That's such a sad book, nobody ends up happy."

She turned to me with what looked like annoyance. Oh great, I had already made an enemy. She turned back to her book, "I know, this is my third time reading it. I find it sad that he couldn't end up with Walter. They were so made for each other, but I guess he needed his space... permanently."

I nodded because I didn't know what else to say. I looked down at my own binder, tracing my fingers over the words I had written. I didn't think she wanted to talk, she seemed so immersed in the book.

"The name's Jenny. I take it you're new to town. I know everyone else in this classroom, we all went to elementary together."

I nodded again, "Just moved from Humboldt. Small town north of here, my parents said something about opportunities or something. So here I am, Levitt high school."

"Smart choice, this school is renowned for its Drama Club. The best in the country. Do you do a lot of acting?"

Not professionally, I thought to myself. I had pretended I was straight for a lot of years, did that count? "Not really, I wanted to be in Drama, but my old school only took paid students, something my parents could never afford. Is it free here or do you have to pay for everything?"

She smiled at me, putting her book down, "My father is really into the arts. He even managed to marry my mother, who is an actress in Vancouver. He gives millions of dollars to the school's drama club, so it's 100% free for everyone. You can even apply for Student Help, which pays for tours or trips we have to do. I'll take you there, I'm going to join this afternoon in my spare after lunch." She looked at her schedule, "Do you have fifth period spare? I guess that's the only way you can come with me."

I took my schedule from my pocket, looking at the times, "I think I do. How do you know if it's a spare?"

She giggled, taking it from my hands, "You do have a fifth period spare! See how it's completely blank? That means you got lucky this year. Most kids beg for their fifth period spare, seeing as it's right after lunch!" She handed the paper back to me, "That's what we'll see then. By the way, are you going anywhere for lunch? I think you'd like to meet my brother, he's big on photography."

I looked around, "Where is your brother, or should I be asking who is your brother?"

"Morgan Winters. He's in grade 12 this year so he'll be leaving next year, but he's a really great guy. You need more friends, and Morgan is one of the best guys I know!" She quickly flashed me a side grin as the teacher walked in and shushed us all. I felt my heart racing, the guy I had met earlier that day was her brother?

"Alright class. Where you are sitting now is where you will be for the rest of the year, so if you want to move, you'll have to do that now. I see a few open chairs of students that couldn't make the first day, so pick wisely." The teacher walked to the whiteboard, scribbling down her name, "I am Ms. Hangstoff."

We all said hello in unison as we opened our binders, and Ms. H looked around the room and smiled, "Let's get to know each other, shall we? We'll start from the left side and work our way back to the other side. I'll start though, seeing as I am a new teacher here."

As we went around the room, everyone seemed friendly enough. They all seemed to know each other though.

I was the new kid in town.

At least I have one friend. Looking over at Jenny, I smiled happily.

Chapter Two

*S*omeone *I never got to know very well was Morgan's best friend, Julian. He seemed like a nice enough fellow at first, but as I got to know his real character, his hard exterior was all for show, and none of it was real. He was like a big, soft teddy bear that just wanted friends. I was his friend, and his support for me and Morgan was insane. He always knew we'd be together.*

I didn't know that Julian was planning on getting us to date for the longest time. I think it just took longer than he would have liked. I found a picture with a date on it. September 4, 2005. As I looked at the picture, I realized it was taken just hours after the lunch one with Jenny. We were talking and walking home when they caught up with us. I took one look at Morgan, and both Jenny and Julian knew I was smitten.

"So tell me about yourself?" she asked as we rounded the corner of the school. Jenny had decided to ask me to come over and meet her parents. "What was your other school like?"

I took a deep breath because I hated when people asked me about my old school. It was like being hit in the stomach with a bat. I hated talking about my old school. "Oh, you know, the regular junior high. Kids being kids I suppose." I looked down at the ground, kicking a pebble I had stumbled upon. I was trying not to make eye contact with her, fearing the tears would start pouring out.

"You got treated pretty badly, didn't you? I'm sorry to see that in your face, I know what bullying is like. The junior high I had was supported greatly by the Windsor Family, who own a lot of small businesses in this town. Their daughter went to school with me, and she was cruel as could be, especially because my family had money but not *as much as her*." She sighed, reaching into her pockets as we walked.

"I came from a very homophobic school, and at the time, I started questioning some stuff. Eventually, they all found out, and I was bullied relentlessly. It was a terrible experience. I moved here hoping all would be better."

She gave me a half-cocked grin, "Are you gay?"

I was about to answer her question when two boys walked out in front of us, with stupid smiles on both their faces. I looked up and recognized Morgan and his friend. They looked down at us and smirked, Morgan holding his camera up to my face.

"Looks like we meet again, Mattie. I see you're with my sister. Were you thinking of getting into her pants and making a baby!?" I couldn't tell if he was joking, I just stood there with a dumb look on my face.

"I-I... no... friends..." I couldn't even talk properly. Part of it was the fact he was accusing me of using a girl to have sex and have a baby with, and the other half was looking into those eyes. I just wanted to look into them all day. "We... walk... parents."

His friend started laughing, "I think he's got a thing for you, Morgie, he can barely keep his sentences together!" A soft punch to Morgan's arm made him start laughing as well, his eyes lighting up slightly.

"Shut up, Julian, you're such an ass. Your first time meeting the poor boy, and you accuse him of liking Morgan! Who would like Morgan anyways, he's a stinky bunch of stinky cheese." Jenny held her hand over her nose to act like a clothespin.

I couldn't help but laugh, my mouth dropping open with her attitude. "Stinky like stinky cheese?" I started laughing harder, trying to stop myself from crying.

Morgan gave us a fake hurt look, his bottom lip trembling slightly, "Well I never! I do not smell like stinky cheese and people like me... I have a fan page! People like what I do, little sis. Try and stop being the lime green jello and deal with it."

I stopped laughing as Jenny pulled me away, "I think it's about time we left these two stinky cheese losers alone. They have things to take pictures of, and we're obviously more important than them! Come on, loverboy, we've got some cookies to eat. I smelt them this morning!"

As we walked away, I could swear I heard Julian and Morgan talking about us, so I walked slower, trying to hear their conversation. "He is really cute, actually. Did you see those adorable dimples? That butt is so cute. I could cuddle that butt."

"You could cuddle anything with a dick, Morgan. Come on, we gotta get to practice before the coach kills us. You can catch up with him later tonight, I'm sure your sister will want him to spend the night or something. What if he isn't even gay? What if we just THINK we saw something, but really... there was nothing."

I desperately wanted to turn around and tell him he was adorable, and I would like to cuddle with him as well. My hand was being dragged further away, and I didn't have a chance to say anything. I looked at the house we were walking up to, and it was huge. There were seven steps to get to the main entrance. Oh my god, I have died and gone to Hollywood heaven!

We walked inside, kicking off our shoes and walking into her bedroom, which looked like a mini apartment.

"I have some Nintendo games if you want to play, but before we do I have a question for you... and you have to be completely honest, okay?"

"Okay...?" I nervously looked at her, trying to see if she was being serious about something or not.

"Mattie, do you think my brother is cute? Would you date him?"

Chapter Three

A picture fell from behind one of the picture frames. I looked at the ground to see a beautiful face staring back at me. Morgan's mother is one of the most interesting people I have ever met. She has dark brown hair that seemed to always be perfect, strong facial features, and she always walked with elegance. I honestly thought she was a model, even though she disagrees to the highest degree. You couldn't help but smile when she was present, she just gave the room light every time.

The picture was taken when she found out her son and I were dating. He said she gave the best facial expression of all time, and he questioned if she would approve. She talked with me more and at the end of the night, exclaimed that she adored me and dating her son would be of the highest privilege. She always talked me up, even if I wasn't the most attractive man in the world.

"So seriously, do you like my brother? I saw the look you gave him when he appeared." She stared at me for a long time, waiting for the answer she wanted to hear.

"Well, we... I..." I was stuttering, nervous as to what she

wanted me to say. I took a deep breath, "He's really cute."

She beamed at me, her white smile giving way to the slight gums it showed, "You think he's cuuuuuuute?"

I started feeling my cheeks turning red, and my ears were burning as I looked away and tried to hide the fact I was blushing pretty hard. I didn't know what to say so I told her the truth, and here she was giving me those stupid eyes. Why did I have to open my big mouth?

The front door opened, and I looked over to see a woman walk into the room and put a briefcase on the counter. She smiled at Jenny and then looked at me, "And who's this?"

Before Jenny or I could answer, the front door opened again, and Morgan and Julian came inside, talking about some concert they were going to. "That's Mattieboy, and he's got a huge crush on your son, Mrs. Winters."

Now I knew I was fifty shades of red. I spluttered at the sudden words coming from Julian's mouth, my jaw dropping in astonishment. What if she didn't know he was gay? I didn't even know if he was gay! What if she disapproved? What if she thought I was crazy and made me leave? I was having a mini panic attack when she smiled in my direction.

"Another caught in Web Morgan, hey? He is pretty cute, for a total slob. Just be careful, he's a biter!" She walked over to Morgan and squeezed his cheek, make them turn a slight tinge of red from the pinching, "But he's not that bad of a kid I suppose. I'm Morgan's mother, in case that wasn't apparent. Do you go to Levitt High, Mathew?"

I cringed. I have always hated when people called me Matthew because it wasn't even my real name! I had to show people my birth certificate all the time to prove it, "Sorry Ma'am, my name is really Mattie, but yes, I'm in Jenny's math class."

She ran her hand over the warm water coming from the faucet, lathering it in soap, "Well that's good! Are you good at math? Maybe you could teach that daughter of mine some math skills so maybe she can pass with more than a fifty percent this year." She gave Jenny a quick glance as Jenny stuck her tongue out.

"Mr. Wonto hated me, you know he did. Maybe if you didn't date him in high school, and then break his heart when you decided to date dad, I would have had better marks!" Jenny just sat pouting in her chair as Morgan started laughing along with his mother, "You screwed me out of a perfect score!"

I was taking in my surroundings, looking around the lavish house. I couldn't believe I was here. I didn't think I could ever bring Jenny to my house because it was a dump compared to this, and it wasn't even a dump. I sighed silently to myself, what I wouldn't give to live in a house like this. "You have a very beautiful house, Mrs. Winters."

Wiping her hands on her dress, she smirked the same smirk I saw on Morgan's face time and time again, "Flattery will get you nowhere boy, but thank you. We built the house a couple years back when both Mr. Winters and I were promoted at work to Head Financial Advisers. I was very particular about how I wanted my house to look, and so after months of searching for something right, we just decided to build it."

Morgan piped up, drowning out his mother, "Well, kiddies, we're going to play some video games upstairs. You're welcome to join us, but only the kiddies. I don't want any old folk stinking up my room." He glanced at his mother with a smile. She rolled her eyes and went to the fridge.

"I don't think I could stand being in that room for more than thirty seconds because it smells like boy and feet. You should really clean it, Morgan."

Before she could finish, he was already up the stairs and laughing with Julian. When I heard a door close, I turned my attention back to Jenny, "So, what are we going to do? Do you want to join them?"

She smirked, "Only in your dreams. Let's go for a walk, I haven't been to the stream in a while." Getting up, she started towards the door, I followed behind, saying goodbye to Mrs. Winters. As we made our way down the path to the river, Jenny was giggling slightly.

I looked at her and sighed, "What seems to be so funny, little miss giggly?"

She turned around, facing me and cupping my face in her small hands, "Guess what?"

"What?" I spat.

"I totally know Morgan likes you back!"

Chapter Four

I met Morgan's father shortly after finding out that he might like me back. I had been spending a considerable amount of time at the Winters' house, playing games with Morgan as well as spending time with Jenny. We had almost become joined at the hip. At first I thought it was just to get closer to him... but after a while I realized I just really liked his family. Carefree and energetic, they were almost the opposite of my career-driven parents.

His father walked into the living room one day when Jenny and I were playing Grand Theft Auto. He sat down beside us and explained how this game was fictitious. He made sure we knew never to really steal a car or have random relations with a hooker and then beat her up for the money we just gave her. Jenny burst out laughing as her father explained the moral implications of the game.

He seemed like a decent man. He looked almost like an older version of Morgan, more refined, but as I thought about it, I liked the way Morgan looked with his carefree hair, his wicked smile and the way he presented himself. I was falling in love with Morgan.

"This game gets boring after a while, when you really stop to think about it. I feel like the missions are almost always the same and honestly, what kind of street gang is this? Why does it always have to be people that are of colour? White people are probably worse." Jenny was trying to explain to me why she sometimes hated this game. I just laughed as she spouted out different information.

"Hey, Snuggles! How are you doing?" A man's voice came from the kitchen, and I felt something touch me as he wrapped his arms around Jenny's shoulders.

"Hey, Daddy! When did you get home? I thought your meetings were until next week!" She got up, grabbing her father and bringing him in for a bear hug.

"They let me out of prison early." He turned his attention to me with the famous Winters smirk coming onto his face, "And who is this fine young gentleman? Is this your new boyfriend your mother is so keen about?"

Jenny gave him a look that could kill, which slightly hurt my feelings, "No! I wouldn't date him! He's trying to get into Morgan's pants. Dad, this is Mattie, he goes to school with me and Morgan."

I felt the sudden rush of red and warmth to my ears. Why did she just say that? This would obviously make things awkward.

Her father gave me a quick look over with the smirk never leaving his face, "Looks better than the rest of them, at least he smells human and not like cheeseburgers or something."

They started laughing, but I didn't get what was going on. I sat there, turning red with every second as they laughed about someone who smelt of cheeseburgers. I turned my attention back to the game, trying hard not to feel embarrassed at the information Jenny was sharing with her father. How could someone be so open about this? My dad would have been so uncomfortable.

"Well, we're thinking of going to Nuit Chanteau for supper tonight." He looked around the room for the clock, finding it resting in the corner, "We're leaving in forty minutes. Are you coming or are video games more important than your father?"

Jenny laughed, "I love that place, I'm for sure coming."

I guess that was my cue to leave. I would never be able to afford anything at Nuit Chanteau, they even charged for water, yes, water! I got up and grabbed my bag from the side of the couch, "Well, have a good supper. Text me tonight, maybe we can finish that calculus homework?" I started towards the door, turning the corner to the stairs when I banged into someone coming down. I rubbed my head as I saw Morgan staring down at me.

"O-o-oh, I'm sorry, M-Morgan!" I looked down at the ground, "I was j-just leaving."

"I heard something about the Nuit! Are we seriously going there?" Morgan walked past me, I quickly took advantage of the situation and made my way towards the door. "I really love their steak and carrots, so good. Hey, Mattieboy, where are you going? Aren't you coming with us?"

I hung my head down in shame, trying to conceal the embarrassment, "Sorry, I c-can't afford the Nuit, I heard it's really expensive."

I heard laughter from that direction, well that sucks. Now they were going to make fun of me for being poor. I had heard this so many times before from people at my old school. I sighed and turned on my heels as I opened the door. I felt someone's hand on my shoulder, and I looked up to see Mr. Winters.

"A friend of Jenny's is a friend of ours. There's no need to be embarrassed; we love treating Jenny's friends to supper. You're more than welcome to come." His smile was so endearing and warm that I couldn't help but slowly back into the house.

"Okay, if it's not too much trouble. I really don't want you to spend money on me."

Another hearty laugh left Mr. Winters' mouth, "Son! When I was younger, my parents had nothing. We were so poor that sometimes I had to wear the same clothes three days in a row. I give to charity all the time, so kids aren't sleeping on the streets, or not eating, or wearing filthy clothes. I'm buying you supper, don't worry at all!"

That made me feel a little bit better, at least he cared about people and wasn't snobby.

Morgan looked over at the door with a smile on his face, "You can sit next to me, Mattieboy. I'd like to get to know you more."

I heard a laugh from the kitchen as Mrs. Winters walked out, "There will be none of that at the table. Leave it for the bedroom!"

Chapter Five

*S*omething extraordinary about Morgan was the way he laughed and how often he laughed. I wouldn't say he would laugh at the inappropriate things in life, but he would laugh when he needed to and when it would lighten the mood. One of my favourite pictures of him was when we were at the county fair. His hair was all over the place as we went on the roller coaster, and our hands were flying around everywhere. Even through all of that, he still managed to take a selfie of both me and him throwing our hands in the air and laughing.

Morgan used to say laughter was the medicine to the cynical parts of life. If you could still laugh, your life wasn't that bad at all. When Morgan was in a room, his laughter was infectious, and everyone would start laughing with him. He would laugh at himself the most, never taking himself too seriously. It was a beautiful thing, and to be completely honest, I think it was one of the things that drew me the closest to him. It was what made me want to be around him all the time, no matter how I was feeling that day.

The car ride was pretty quiet. Julian had also decided to

invite himself on the dinner trip, but the Winters were more than welcoming to let another passenger aboard their car. I sighed as I sat in the back of the minivan they had bought, right next to Morgan. My palms were sweating, and I didn't know how to talk. In front of us, Julian and Jenny were giggling and joking around while Mr. and Mrs. Winters talked in the front about classical music.

As I looked out the window, I felt something on my hand. I looked down to see Morgan shuffling his hand over mine, and our fingers entwining as we rode to the restaurant. I was sweating heavily and was nervous about him putting his hand on mine, but he just smiled and mouthed a *calm down*. I took a few deep breaths and let him gently touch my hand, running his fingers over the webbing.

I shivered slightly at the sensation, as I had never had someone touch me so romantically before. It felt right, having his hand entwined with mine, his soft fingers doing magic on my rough hands. The ride was too short because before I knew it, everyone was getting out of the car, Morgan included. I just wanted to sit there and hold his hand for as long as possible. I sighed heavily but gave way to peer pressure and stepped out of the car.

My foot accidentally caught the side of the door, and I stumbled out of the car and right into Morgan's arms. He smirked down at me as I turned red and stuttered something incoherent about not knowing how to walk. Jenny gave me a mild smirk as she shook her head. I didn't mean to do it. Why was everyone giving me that look?

"Morgan loves the whole Damsel in Distress thing. Good job, Mattie, maybe he'll like you more that way. He'll think he has to protect you or something." Jenny teased as we walked into Nuit. I was traumatized, and everyone was snickering about it, even Morgan.

As it turned out, the Winters were regulars at the place, and so within minutes, we were sitting on the veranda with drinks already on the table. I sat next to Morgan, who smiled at me and quickly put his hand back on mine, just where I wanted it.

"Welcome back, folks, it's nice to see your shining faces again! I see we have a new addition to the regular team. I'm Mandy, and these folks ask for me every time they come though I don't know why I'm so popular! What's your name?"

"Mattie." I squeaked it out, trying to hold in the excitement of having a regular server.

"Are you Morgan's new boytoy? I hear he's a hard one to catch," she winked at him.

Smiling, Morgan bowed his head, "You're just missing an extremity I kind of like, Mandy. Sorry!"

They laughed slightly as she walked away with our order. I could feel everyone staring at me, and it made me slightly uncomfortable, but Morgan's hand entwined in mine made me calm down slightly. Our food was there within what seemed like minutes, hot and fresh, I felt my stomach growling to consume this food.

Halfway through our meal, Morgan dropped a meatball onto his lap from his spaghetti. Everyone looked over to see him doing a little dance as he flung it to the ground. Before anyone else could start, Morgan was laughing hysterically at himself and picking the meatball up with a napkin. He started singing, and everyone else joined in laughing.

"I dropped my poor meatball, all covered in sauce..."

Sitting back down, I finished my meal and rubbed my stomach. That food was absolutely amazing. We ate dessert and then headed out with some takeout, the food here was too filling for anyone to finish all in one go. We made our way back to the van, sitting in our normal seats. We started driving, and the familiar feeling of a hand on mine returned. Why was he being so touchy with me all of a sudden? Not that I was complaining, it was just out of the blue.

We drove through the streets and up to the house, I looked at my watch and starting freaking out, "Oh gosh! I need to get home. I bet my family is wondering when I'll be back or something." I picked out my phone and dialed my parents' number, getting my mother on the other line. Before I could talk, Morgan whispered in my ear.

"Stay the night with me?"

I gulped, "Hey, Mommy, can I stay the night at the Winters'? They'll drive me to school tomorrow? I promise not to be late!"

Without even so much as an argument, she told me to be safe.

Chapter Six

Everyone always used to say we made the cutest couple of all time. I found a picture of us curled together in a ball on the couch. My face was buried in his chest as a scary movie played in the background. He loved taking pictures of us. He loved seeing my face and reaction every time his camera was out in the open.

I liked the attention, but I wasn't used to it. I had gone from being virtually unknown to everyone in school talking about the boy that got Morgan Winters. I guess I should have been happier about it, but I didn't know we would last as long as we did. I just reveled in the moments we had shared. I felt closer to him, and I loved every moment of it. I loved when he wrapped his arms around me and pulled me into a hug. I found he did it more and more often, always holding on for a little longer. I guess that meant he loved me, but I knew nothing of love.

I didn't even know love could exist, but he knew and apparently so did the rest of his family. I got invited out more and more each week until it was almost like I was a second son.

"Hey, Mattieboy, wanna watch a movie with me and

Julian? I think Jenny would also be into it. It's a scary movie though." He wrapped his arm around my shoulder as we walked in the door, "Don't worry, I'll protect you."

I looked around the house. I hated scary movies, but I guess I could handle it just for tonight. I'd be watching it with Morgan, and maybe it would give me an excuse to cuddle up with him and not seem desperate, "Okay, but if I get scared, you need to hold me."

He just laughed that beautiful laugh and walked into the den, which was attached to the living room. As I walked inside, I was amazed by all the gadgets. A big screen television lined the wall. A couch stood in the middle of the room, and it seemed like the most comfortable thing in the world. The wall was covered with old movie posters that were worn out and some new ones of recent movies.

"I just realized I don't have a change of clothes! I'm going to have to go home after this. I need to smell fresh tomorrow." I looked at Morgan, whispering under my breath, "Sorry."

He just smiled at me, "Don't worry, I've got some spare clothes from when I was a bit younger, so you can just fit into those. Now, get on that couch, and we'll start the movie." He closed the blinds to block the sunlight from the screen. Then he put on the movie and came back to sit next to me on the couch.

Within twenty minutes, I was curled into a ball on his chest. I was honestly trying to watch the movie, but I kept shrieking every time something happened. Morgan, Julian, and Jenny were all laughing at me. It was obvious they were trying to hold in some extreme laughter, but I couldn't help myself. I really did not like horror movies. They always made me feel so out of place with everyone, because I was the scared little boy.

I felt Morgan's arms grip me tighter, his lips stretching into that classic smirk of his, "Don't worry, Mattieboy. I'm here. Nobody's going to get you."

Small words, big actions. Even if he didn't know it, at this point, I was already falling in love with him. I felt so safe in his embrace like nobody was going to hurt me. I knew if I stayed here, no matter what happened, I would always be safe. It made the movie less scary, and I could tolerate it all the way through.

The movie finished up, and Julian started stretching, "Well, I guess I should be going. You two lovebirds have fun tonight, don't do anything I wouldn't do."

Morgan snickered, "Don't worry, we'll be doing what you do every night. Jack off to some porn and cry yourself to sleep without a woman."

Julian grumbled something as he walked out of the room, flipping Morgan off, which just made all of us laugh even harder. Getting off the couch, I looked around the room, "So I guess I can sleep here, right?"

Morgan grabbed my hand, "Are you kidding me? I've got a spot right next to me in bed."

I was flustered, was he really suggesting that I sleep with him in the same bed? I didn't really have a choice since he just started pulling me towards his room, completely ignoring my resistance.

"I...I... we... I." I couldn't talk, and I was getting closer to his room. I needed to think of an excuse, but nothing was coming to my head. I did want to sleep with him in the same bed, but what if it lead to something else? What if I let myself go!

"Here we go, my bedroom!" He seemed proud of his room, and I was just in awe. It was huge, it could have been the size of a two bedroom apartment. The walls were covered with band posters as well as some framed pictures I assumed he had taken. His bed was in the middle of the room. It was a circular bed with drapes around it. In the corner of my eye, I saw the dark room where he must have developed his pictures. This was beautiful.

"This is where you sleep. Wow."

He just smiled as he ran his hands over objects throughout the room, "It's pretty big. Sometimes I wish I had a smaller room, but my parents said I needed a dark room, so it's over there. It gets kind of lonely in here, you know?"

All I could do was nod. I hadn't expected him to feel the emotion of lonely. I thought he had everyone fawning over him at school.

My thoughts were interrupted by his hands running along my chest as he was looking into my eyes. What was he doing? "Hey, Mattieboy. Would it be okay if I kissed you?"

Chapter Seven

As the year was ending, our school took us on a school-wide trip. We went to a swimming pool near the school. Everyone came to swim, talk, and enjoy the time before we all said goodbye to our seniors. Morgan had naturally brought his camera with him and was sneaking pictures of me without me even knowing.

I found one of them stuffed in the bottom of the box. I was wearing red shorts and was laughing at something Jenny had done. It was a genuine laugh, and knowing Morgan, he always wanted me to remember what I looked like when I actually smiled. He should have known when I was around him, my smiles were always real. He always made me laugh, and I felt like when I smiled around him, it actually meant something.

As I flipped it over, I realized the picture had something written on the back. I read the words slowly and carefully.

"He's always the most beautiful when he laughs. The way his cheeks puff out, and he can't stop from slapping his knee is amusement."

I sighed, he really did know the best parts about me, more than anyone else in the world did.

I sat with my feet in the cold water, and the refreshing feeling engulfed me. It might have only been April, but the balmy weather was already starting to come into the small town. A Chinook had made itself known, and the snow that had once littered every part of the town was slowly disappearing. We all knew it wouldn't last. We all knew another snow storm was coming, but for now, we were all wondering if we could stand the heat.

Our school had rented out one of the local swimming pools, and the entire school was present. Everyone seemed to be enjoying each other's presence, even if some of the older kids just sat on the sidelines, texting on their phones and ignoring the pleas of the teachers to join in on the festivities. Morgan wasn't one of them. He was splashing with his sister and Julian by the deep end. I could see Jenny's head splashing in and out of the water, barely tall enough to reach the floor.

"Are you going to join us or am I going to have to come over there and get you myself?" His voice came from the water, I just smiled and shook my head no. He smirked at me and started walking through the water to me. I squealed as he grabbed my legs and pulled me into the water.

I splashed him as I tried to swim away, but he had other plans for me. His arms wrapped around my torso, and he pulled me into an embrace with our lips lightly touching as we stood in the water. I tried to get away, but he was pressed against me, not letting me go from this spot.

"I told you you needed to have fun, Mattieboy. You need to lighten up, have some fun, and get out of this silly funk you're in."

"I'm not in a funk. I just don't enjoy swimming as much as the rest of you. I'm actually getting hungry, and I was thinking of hitting the snack stand." I moved away from him and started reaching for the ladder. I felt his hands beside me, pulling himself out of the water. "I guess you can join me if that's what you'd like."

He just smiled as he walked beside me. I was getting nervous about him being there. I couldn't tell you what it was, but there was just something about him that made me sweat. I just wanted the feeling to go away, even if it made me giddy knowing someone made me feel that way. Then he grabbed my hand and continued walking beside me.

He was holding my hand. In. public... in front. of. EVERYONE. Oh my god.

I shot glances around the pool, but I didn't see anyone looking at us. They all seem preoccupied with the fun of swimming. I calmed down slightly, but I still had to stare and make sure nobody was judging me.

"What are you going to have?" He was so oblivious to what I was feeling that it was actually kind of cute.

I looked at the menu as we walked up to the snack shop. He dropped his hands from mine, making me sigh slightly. "How about a hot dog?"

"I've got a hot dog for you, alright."

I looked at him with a dumb look, "Where did you get a hot dog without me?"

He started laughing, and then it clicked in.

Oh... my... god. I started blushing a few million shades of red. I put my face into my hands, a slight smirk on my face. I can't believe he just made a dirty joke, and I didn't get it. I thought I was the king of dirty. I took a deep breath and nodded, indicating I wanted a hot dog... either the one from the shop or the one from his pants, I wasn't being picky.

He stifled his laugh and ordered our food, taking it to one of the nearby tables. As we sat and ate, he looked at me every so often.

"What?"

"Mattieboy, have I ever told you how beautiful you are?"

I looked down at the ground, trying to be as quiet as I could, "Nobody has ever called me beautiful before."

The first time I saw him truly frown was at that moment. He looked around and sighed, "Well, you are probably the most gorgeous boy I have ever seen, and I've seen a lot. Do you want to stay the night with me again? We can play some video games or something?"

I looked at him as I tried to figure him out. Did he actually want to spend more time with me? I would have assumed he wouldn't want to spend that much more with me. "Yea, if you want me to?"

He just smiled, "Good. We can cuddle again."

I looked at him and smiled, God... why is he so perfect?

Chapter Eight

*H*is hair had to be one of the most interesting things about Morgan. He was one of the only people in the world that I knew of that could pull off the messy bed hair all the time. He never combed it, and I wouldn't have been surprised if he found a rat's nest growing in there one morning. It always seemed to be spiked up in multiple positions, never really lying straight anywhere, but it looked good. It was crazy and wild, just like Morgan on some days.

As crazy as he was, Morgan was also sweet and caring. I'd fall asleep lying in his arms every night with the feeling of his warmth radiating on my skin. I loved lying around with him, even if it was just watching a movie and giggling over what was happening. I felt like my life was almost a comedy, but the feeling of being with him made me feel like I could laugh at life.

I remember waking up one morning as he was taking a selfie in the mirror, and I couldn't stifle the laugh that came out. When I asked him about it, he just shrugged and smiled, bringing his camera over to us and taking a picture of us in bed. The moment was perfect, even if I *didn't look amazing with bed hair.*

"What are you doing, Morgan?" I yawned and stretched as he took a few pictures, posing in the mirror in his underwear. I started laughing at his facial expressions, "I've noticed you do this every morning."

"I need to see what I look like every morning, we're all getting older, Mattieboy. I want to see myself transform from the young kid I was to the old guy I'll end up being. I want to see what aged first, which will probably be my eyes or something. My mom had hawk eyes, I assume I'll end up with them as well."

I laughed, "Hawk eyes? What the hell are those?"

He walked over to the bed, crawling back in beside me with his camera poised above us, "Say cheese."

I was about to protest when the flash clicked, and I closed my eyes, a small grin on my face. I turned on my side, propping my elbow on the bed as I rested my head in my hand. His chest moved slowly up and down, and with every movement, I saw his nose flare. I could watch him for as long as he'd let me, everything about him just made my heart flutter.

He caught me this time, "What are you looking at exactly?" He turned his head to the side, and a smirk formed on his lips.

"I... you..." I covered my face with my hands, as embarrassment overcame my emotions, "I was just looking at how amazing you look."

He shuffled over beside me, and his arm wrapped around my back, pulling me into his chest, "You're just as amazing to look at, Mattieboy. I think you need to see what I see when I look at you." Pulling out his camera again, he flipped through some pictures of me. I was blushing, I really didn't want to see these pictures. "You have this infectious smile, and you always put a smile on my face. Even when you try giving me a grumpy face, which rarely ever looks grumpy."

I looked at him with my brows furrowing as I pouted, "I can be grumpy."

He just laughed, kissing me as he put the camera down, "You can never be grumpy. Who do you think you are? You're just this little adorable ball of cute."

I had nothing, so I just let myself find comfort in his arms. Stealing kisses ever so often, I lay on his chest and drifted off, letting sleep overtake me for yet another few hours. It was pleasant, and I loved lying there with him, even if it was the middle of the morning.

I woke up to the sun high in the sky, looking at the clock I noticed it was now three in the afternoon. Morgan grunted as he woke up, smiling at me. "Well, are we going to get up now? I think my stomach might eat itself if I don't put some food in it."

I giggled slightly, "Yea, do you want me to make you something?"

He thought for a second, "You know what? I have a better idea, let me take you on a date. I've almost seen you naked, but I've never taken you out on a proper date. Maybe we should do that, want to go get some food and go on a date?"

I could tell I wouldn't be able to say no since he looked so excited about his whole idea. I guess we could go on a date. It was Saturday, and I guess that meant I would be able to stay out late. I should probably go home tonight though, I've stayed here three nights in a row, but for some reason I don't think my parents would even notice I was gone.

"Sure, that sounds like a plan. Where are we going to go?"

He went into thinking mode again, and he looked so adorable when he thought really hard. I wouldn't call him stupid, but he definitely wasn't the sharpest knife in the drawer. He smiled down at me, "Well, we can't go to the Nuit, that's a family thing. How about we go to Denny's, it's low-key, and they have some amazing pancakes. I love pancakes."

I just giggled and got up, "What shall I wear?"

He got up and walked to the closet, "Something stunning. Should we dress up in suits and pretend we're business people?"

"That sounds ridiculous, but also super fun, let's do this!"

He gave me an old suit and grabbed his own, slipping all the components on. Apparently, I couldn't see him until he was done getting ready, I sighed, "Are you ready yet?"

"Yep." He walked out of the closet, and my jaw dropped.

And here I thought he couldn't get even more gorgeous.

Chapter Nine

*A*s I made another sift through the photo box sitting on my lap, I found the pictures I thought had long been thrown away. Morgan had a dirty mind, but he surprised me one day after a few weeks of dating with naked pictures of himself. At first, I thought they were a gag gift, he had photoshopped himself on some model's body, but I soon realized by the disappointment on his face they were, in fact, of him. At least I thought they were a model's body!

Nostalgia ran through my body as I remembered every single curve of his body, something I would never forget. He had an amazing body, even if some would have looked down upon it. He wasn't rocking some killer abs, and he wasn't throwing muscle out the window. He had a bit of a belly, but it was cute, like a teddy bear. He also had skinny arms and skinny legs, but they all worked well together. I thought he was beautiful, more beautiful than those models you saw in the movies.

I couldn't keep my eyes off him after seeing those pictures, something inside of me just wanted more. So on a rainy day in September, I made my move. It was the first of many, but I had finally found the courage *to love him and show him I loved him.*

We were sitting in the field, watching the stars burning brightly in the sky. I had never just sat under the stars and watched them, but Morgan had convinced me, saying they all had a story to tell. He went on about how each star was actually no longer alive. They had burst in galaxies far away. I always thought that was a myth. If it was true, then how was it possible that there were millions of stars in the sky every night?

I just put my head on his chest and watched, amused by the way he talked about them. He drew out some of the constellations with his hand, something I didn't even know about. The big dipper seemed to be one of the most prominent ones, but he said every night was different. I loved when he talked about these kinds of things because it made me feel less like a nerd when someone else knew smart stuff.

The first few droplets started later on in the night, but we ignored them for the comfort we were giving each other. My face was getting slightly damp, but soon it was no longer sprinkling. The rain started pouring down, we both flung up out of our spot and started running towards the car. Screaming the entire way, I tried opening the door to get inside, but the door was locked.

"MORGAN! Open the door, I'm getting soaked out here! Hurry up!" My clothes were soaking wet from the downpour, and I looked back only to find that I could not see him anywhere. That's when I started to panic. "MORGAN!"

I felt someone wrap their arms around me and before I knew it, his lips were pressed against mine, our wet clothes sticking together as he passionately kissed me against the car. Even though I was slightly uncomfortable, I let him continue. Everyone always talked about kissing in the rain, but I really didn't know how romantic and amazing it was until it was happening to me.

Our fingers entwined as we continued to kiss, our bodies moving together in rhythm. He unlocked the doors with the key fob and opened the door, gesturing for me to get in. I quickly jumped inside, before taking my wet sweater off and tossing it in the back. As Morgan got inside, he quickly turned the car on then cranked up the heat.

"That was..." I couldn't finish my sentence, I was just so amused by what had happened, I wondered if it would ever happen again.

"You're a really good kisser, I think you've had practice." His legendary smirk came out as he teased me, giving me a look.

I just laughed, because I didn't know what to say. I could have lied, but he really was the first boy I had ever kissed. He tasted like bubble gum and taffy, a weird combination, but it worked for him. I always envisioned he would taste like cotton candy, mainly because I thought he was so sweet and cotton candy was always my favourite sweet thing to eat. I was wrong, but it wasn't really a problem.

"We should probably get home soon and take a hot shower to heat ourselves up. I didn't really think about it while you were standing there, but I guess hypothermia is a problem." He laughed lightly, but my thoughts were somewhere else because that kiss had really been amazing. It was at that moment, I think I fell in love with him. I had never felt this way about anyone and even though it had only been a few weeks, I wanted him around all the time. Maybe my parents would even like him, if not anyone else.

"Morgan... pull the car over."

He gave me a look, but I just repeated myself. He looked kind of nervous, "Is everything alright?"

"Just... just pull the car over." I couldn't second guess myself now, it was now or never.

He pulled the car over and, without second guessing

myself, I pulled him into the back of the car. It was clumsy and sloppy, but amazing. My hands ran through his hair with my fingers caressing his scalp as I kissed him, pushing his body against the window. I just wanted him right now, and I wanted him all to myself, no compromising.

The next thing I remember doing was taking his shirt off, kissing his neck as I did so. My hands found each and every curve of his body, and it was at this moment I realized I was hungry.It was the hunger of wanting, needing to be as close to him as possible boiling within me like a craving I had been feelingthis entire time finally erupting in a way I couldn't control. Within a few minutes, we were both naked, with him lying on top of me. He smirked down at me, "Are... are we really doing this?"

I wanted to stop myself but at the same time I didn't want to stop anything.

I just wrapped my legs around his waist.

"Make love to me, Morgan."

Chapter Ten

I can't remember if Morgan and I ever had a big fight. We really were calm and collected people, and the idea of a new relationship didn't make us mad; it made us giggly and cute. We were falling in love and doing everything new couples usually did. We were holding hands, kissing passionately, giggling to each other. We were always together, never wanting to be apart. Nothing about him bothered me, and nothing he did ever made me mad. He always used to tell me I was his one and only and that we'd never fight because he loved me so much.

I knew eventually the feeling would subside, and we would in fact fight about something, whether it be the littlest thing or the worst thing I could think of. For now, we just lived in the bliss of knowing that neither one of us could live without the other, even if only for a few hours.

I found a picture of the day after we first made love. I had the goofiest smile on my face, and I think I was the happiest guy alive. Every single time someone would say something about how I looked so happy, I would just smile and nod, trying to keep my emotions on the down-low for at least a little longer. Once you start telling people someone is your boyfriend... it usually means something bad is going to happen.

I was awoken by the light shining into the car, and my muscles tightened as I realized where I was and what we were doing. My head shot up, glaring out the windows for anyone that might have walked past the car and looked inside. My heart was beating a million beats per second as I watched for any sign to tell me someone saw.

I felt his arm reach around and pull me back down, and I winced at the slight sun coming into the backseat of the car. He mumbled as he spoke, covering his eyes with his free hand, "Tinted windows, nobody can see in, we can only see out."

I calmed down a little bit, pushing myself back into his arms. The feeling only stayed for a few seconds until I realized I was wearing absolutely nothing on my body. I grimaced as I grabbed my shirt, pulling it on my body, trying to cover every part up with something. I looked around the car for the rest of my clothes, getting up slightly.

"What are you doing? Can't a guy get a few more winks of sleep?" A smirk danced on his lips, but I didn't notice as I scrambled to cover myself.

"I'm... I'm naked! I don't have a stitch of clothing on. This is absolutely terrible, and I'm sorry you have to see this. I should have thought this over more."

His hand went from caressing my arm to smacking it, actually quite hard. I winced a little as he tossed my clothes back on the floor. He wrapped his arm around me and held me down, "You have nothing to hide, every inch of you is beautiful."

I blushed and turned my head into his armpit, I was trying my hardest not to squeal in happiness. What was wrong with this guy? Why was he so romantic? Guys were not supposed to be like this.

Hours passed and finally we decided to get dressed and head back home, well to his home at least. His parents might worry that we got caught in the thunderstorm last night, but with no text messages from anyone, I thought it might just be a safe bet they assumed we were doing something else... somewhere else. For part of it, they were correct. I'd assume they didn't think we'd be doing that in the back of his car, probably somewhere else.

As we drove back to the house, he wasn't talking, and it made me kind of nervous. I had just had an amazing night, one that I was sure to remember for a very long time, but he wasn't talking about it. To make matters worse, he had just taken my virginity, I could handle him ignoring me if I hadn't just let that go.

"So... did you have a good time?"

He smirked, not taking his eyes off the road. "It was a good night."

I fiddled with my thumbs, trying to think of some type of conversation. I might have seemed moderately calm on the outside, but inside I was panicking. What if he told me he never wanted to see me again?

"I think you should go home tonight though, we've been spending a lot of time together lately." He pulled into the driveway.

I was about to lose it, and I could feel tears burning to be let out. He didn't want to spend the night with me? What the hell was happening? "Oh... uh... yea..." I awkwardly unbuckled my seat belt and opened the door, getting out into the driveway. I started walking home, shaking and confused. I couldn't believe this was happening. What did I do wrong?

As I made my way down the sidewalk, holding in the tears and kicking a pebble I found, I thought of everything that had happened. I would never be able to come over again because it would be much too awkward with Morgan around. Had he really used me for his own sexual gratification? I suddenly felt dirty.

Before I turned the corner, I felt someone's hands on me, I turned around to see Morgan staring at me, a smile on his lips, "I just don't want your parents to worry. You can come over after school tomorrow, okay?"

My mood brightened up, "Okay! I can do that."

He bent down and hugged me, our lips touching for a quick second. I felt his hands touching my back lightly, and I shivered as soon as he touched me.

He put his mouth to my ear and whispered, "I love you, Mattieboy."

Chapter Eleven

*M*y parents were never pro-gay, but they weren't homophobic either. I think the biggest hurdle for me was the fact they really wanted a grandchild, and they weren't completely supportive of the idea of adoption. Any boyfriend they were introduced to was met with rejection. Until they met Morgan.

The first day he met my mother, it was two in the morning. I had gotten home from his house, and the little bastard couldn't sleep without me, so he ended up at my house. I found a picture of him and her together, smiles all around. I never expected anyone to make my mother smile that way again, especially a guy that I was seeing.

I should have known that eventually he would meet her, and with the way he was, it should have been obvious my mother would have loved him. He just had this way of making everyone around him comfortable, even if they didn't like the gay aspect of his life. When he showed up at my door, the scene that unfolded was something I never would have expected. Slowly but surely, I learned that was Morgan Winters, and expecting the unexpected was the first page in the *handbook of his love.*

I walked into the house. It was quiet, and the lights were mainly off, except in my parents' bedroom. I quietly crept up the stairs, trying to make it into my room before they even noticed, but I forgot about the last step. As I put pressure on it, the sound of creaking wood resonated throughout the upstairs.

"Mattie, is that you?" I heard my mother calling, well so much for being ninja and getting into bed without a fight.

"Yes, mama, it's me." I poked my head into the bedroom, noticing my father still wasn't home, that was weird.

She patted the spot next to her, and I crept into the room, sitting on the edge of the bed. She looked really mad, and I knew this would end terribly. I wasn't really in the mood to explain myself, but I guess I really needed to get this over with. Eventually, she would find out about my life, and that would just make it worse. I sighed, looking into her eyes.

"You've been gone for a few days now, where have you been hiding?" She put her book down on the nightstand and looked at me, I took a deep breath.

"I've been spending time at the Winters' with Jenny." I lied, not wanting to include the idea that I was with her brother the entire time.

"Oh, it's nice to see you've made a friend in that school. Does she have any siblings or is she the only child?"

Before I could answer, I heard a knock at the door. Oh my god, who the hell was knocking at this hour. My mother looked out the door, confusion etched on her face. She nodded towards the door, "Can you get that? Whoever it is, tell them it's two in the morning and that is absolutely not a time to be coming to someone's house."

I nodded, getting off the bed and walking downstairs. I walked to the door and turned on the outside light, opening the door a crack to see Morgan standing on the porch. He was swaying back and forth, and he looked super nervous.

As he should be, he was knocking on my door at two in the morning.

"What are you doing here, Morgan?" I whispered, hoping my mother wouldn't be able to hear this conversation.

"I missed you. I couldn't sleep, I just kept looking beside me, wondering why you weren't with me. I should have told you to stay, I just had to see your face, that's all. I'm sorry for coming so late. I just really wanted to see your beautiful face. I can go now, can I just have a kiss?" He looked sheepish, and I had to admit that it was adorable, even if it was early in the morning.

"Okay, but then you have to go! My mother will lose her mind if she sees you around here." I leaned out the door, he grabbed my face with his hands and pressed his lips to mine, kissing me as passionately as the last time. I moaned slightly at the emotions running through my brain, but they were cut off early when I heard my mother's voice calling from the stairs.

"What's going on here? Who is this, Mattie?"

I turned around, and sweat started gathering on the top of my forehead. How was I going to explain this? I started stuttering as nervousness took over me completely. What was I going to say? I just stood there, watching her like a hawk.

"You must be the mother Mattie is always talking about, I'm sorry to come here so late, I just needed to see Mattie. My name is Morgan, and I'm Jenny Winters' older brother." Morgan smiled, waving at her awkwardly.

Oh god, here we go, this was going to be absolutely the worst day of my life. I was going to be grounded from going to Jenny's house for a month after this.

"Oh, he talks about me all the time? What kind of things does he say?" She looked inquisitively at him, and I was starting to panic.

"I tried getting him to stay at my house tonight, but he

said he needed to see you because he missed you a lot. He's always going off about how beautiful you are, and how he's pretty sure he inherited all your traits instead of his father's. I must say, he does have a point, you look young enough to be his sister."

For the first time in years, I heard my mother stutter as she ran her fingers through her hair. Was she... nervous? She motioned for him to come in, "Want a cup of tea, I would love to know you better."

"Absolutely." He walked in and shut the door.

Was this seriously happening now?

Chapter Twelve

*M*y *mother was the easy one to get along with. Even if she didn't accept a lot of things, she was the open one of my parents. She loved meeting all my friends, and she loved getting to know the life I was living. My father, he was on the other spectrum of life. He was reserved and quiet, always working. He never asked to meet my friends, and he just wanted me to stay out of his way. He loved me, he just didn't really enjoy parenthood. I think he just wanted someone to continue the bloodline, too bad his only son ended up gay.*

When my mother started talking about Morgan, he all of a sudden had an interest in my friends and love life. He wanted to meet this Morgan, but I really didn't want him to. I really just wanted to keep Morgan all to myself and let my parents pretend I would one day meet a girl and get married. That little image was shattered when my mother told my father I was dating some guy and she just "absolutely loved him." So my father insisted we invite Morgan over for supper. I thought this was going to be an absolute disaster.

The day was progressing faster than I would have wanted.

Staring at the wall clock in my bedroom, I realized that Morgan would be here sooner rather than later, and I really didn't want him to meet the man I called my father. It's not that I didn't love my father, I really do. Meeting Morgan will just confirm this whole thing, he'll never have his bloodline passed on and I don't want to see the look of disappointment in his eyes when the realization sets in. He was downstairs cooking dinner with my mother while I did some homework and each passing second filled me with dread, knowing exactly what was to come.

When my phone started vibrating, I looked down at the caller display and smiled, well at least he's calling me before he leaves. I answered the phone, trying to sound as optimistic as possible, "Hey, Morgan."

After a brief silence, he finally answered me, "Hey, Babe, what's your dad's favourite sport?" I was a little stunned by two things, one was the fact he called me Babe, and the second was his question. "It's hockey, isn't it? Canadians love hockey, right?"

I rolled my eyes, "So do Americans, Morgan." I took a deep breath, "I think hockey is his favourite sport, I don't know, I don't really pay attention when it's on the television. He gets into any sport really, and he's super competitive."

"Oh, okay! Well anyways, I'm heading over in five minutes, is supper ready?"

I sighed, "Yes, it should be ready in about ten minutes. I'll see you then, *probably for the last time.*" I whispered the last part, but Morgan didn't seem to hear me since his cheery demeanor was still hanging on the other line.

"Okay, Mattieboy! I'll see you soon." He hung up the phone, and my heart started beating even faster. I can't believe he was coming to meet my parents. They never met any boyfriends... this was going to be terrible.

I huffed quietly to myself and regained my composure, then walked down the stairs, yelling as nonchalantly as possible, "Morgan'll be here in five."

"Are you going to set the table? We're almost done here." I heard my mother yell from the kitchen. They were trying to make something special if they were both cooking. Either that or they were poisoning the food, II couldn't be quite sure.

As I set the table, I looked around the room, my mom had cleaned like I had never seen before. Everything was shining, you could even see the fact she had revarnished the cupboards. Well, that's awkward. Were they nervous about meeting one of my friends? I mean, my mother really talked up Morgan, but it wasn't that big of a deal, was it?

Before I could ask them about their sudden interest in cleaning, I heard the doorbell ring. *Oh god, he's here.* I took a deep breath and walked towards the door, my parents close behind me. That was kind of creepy, so I shot them a glare and they backed off. Yea, I'm sure my boyfriend would love coming to my house with my parents looming over the door. Way to make him feel welcome, guys.

I opened the door, not really prepared for what I was going to see. A tight-fitted black v-neck clung to his body, dark wash skinny jeans clung to his legs, and high tops adorned his feet. He had some weird necklace on, and he looked like a completely different person... except for his hair. That still remained a collection of a mess. It made me feel slightly less anxious, knowing he was still the same Morgan I loved, just an obvious attempt to impress my parents.

"Hey," I quietly said as I opened the door more.

"Hey, Mattieboy." He smiled as he walked in, "And you must be the parents I have heard so much about. It's nice to finally see you in the light, Mrs. Hawkins." He kissed her hand, something I never knew could possibly be awkward, "And you must be his father, Mr. Hawkins. I'm hoping we can catch the Sharks game tonight; they're my favourite team."

My father stood there for a second blinking slightly, "That's my favourite team as well! That's wonderful, it's on at eight tonight, right?"

Morgan let a small smile form on his face, "Actually, from what I understand they bumped it up an hour, so the game should be starting at seven. Perhaps we should eat quickly so we can catch the start." Jamming his fork into the food, Morgan took a quick bite, looked back up at my parents with surprise, "But that shouldn't be a problem. This supper looks and tastes absolutely amazing. I assume it's a joint effort of the both of you?"

My mother laughed, *a real laugh*, "We both worked on supper together. He cooked the meat, and I made the salad and dessert. I hope you're not a vegetarian because we barbecued some steaks and ribs."

I watched as they walked into the kitchen, talking like they had known each other for a very long time. I stood there, completely stunned by how well they were getting along already. I took a deep breath and made my way to the kitchen, where my mother was looking in the fridge for something to drink. Morgan and my father were sitting at the kitchen table... and they were talking about football now.

I couldn't help but smile, maybe this wouldn't be so bad.

Chapter Thirteen

I don't know how he did it, but Morgan blew away any expectations I had of that night. He impressed both my parents, which I did not expect to happen. He could go from talking about the latest news article with my mother to score comparing of the latest hockey game with my father. Everything seemed to flow naturally with their conversation. I just sat there, taking it all in and smiling ever so often. This was fantastic. Finally, I had someone both my parents could agree was a good fit for me. Maybe they would start accepting the fact I wasn't going to continue the Hawkins bloodline as they wanted, but maybe adopting them with Morgan would be an acceptable solution.

Then, as we finished dinner and started working on dessert, my mother dropped the bomb of a question. I never expected the words to come out of her mouth, but as she asked, my mouth hung open in surprise. I immediately got red and started looking around the room as I tried to find an escape from the situation, but there was nowhere to go. I couldn't just leave Morgan to fend for himself against my hungry parents. I went to interject, but without missing a beat... Morgan *seemed to have every angle covered.*

"So, Morgan, I have a serious question for you. You seem like a nice boy, but I just need to ask because this relationship with my son seems to have progressed pretty quickly. Have you and Mattie had sex?" My mother and father both turned their attention to Morgan as I sat there, stunned to silence.

Oh my god, she just dropped the s word... they just met! Oh my god, how the hell was this happening? What was he going to say? I turned to Morgan, fear engulfing my eyes as he smiled, please do not tell them we have! They'll never let me see you again!

"Mattieboy here has made it very clear that he doesn't really want to do that until he knows I'm sticking around for a while. He's a virgin, and I think his virginity means a lot to him. He doesn't want to give it to just anybody. That makes me happy he thinks highly enough of himself, I think it shows real character. Obviously, he got that from his parents."

I looked back from my mother to my father, were they going to buy it? Oh god, they had to. They could not know we had sex, but the look on Morgan's face was confident, oh god...

Surprisingly, my father was the first one to break this awkward silence, "We always told Mattie he needed to have some self-respect. I'm so glad to hear he that he has kept his legs shut." Getting up from the table, my father grabbed the dishes and headed to the dishwasher, but before he could start loading it, Morgan grabbed the dishes.

"You guys worked hard to cook, let me and Mattieboy here take care of the dishes. Why don't you meet me in the living room? We can catch the game in a few minutes."

My father stood there for a second with a stunned looked on his face, "But... you're a guest. So..."

Morgan cut him off, "It's quite alright. That's the rule in

my house, whoever cooks does not do the dishes. Seeing as both you and the missus cooked, it's only right for me and Mattieboy to do the dishes. So please, find a seat on the couch, and we'll be there soon."

My father smiled and took a step back, before heading into the living room with my mother. I let out a deep sigh of relief that we were finally alone, and walked over to the sink to soak the pots and pans. Morgan filled the dishwasher and put away everything else, opening the cupboards to see where it went. I started washing the dishes when he came up behind me, wrapping his arms around my waist.

"So, was that a top notch act or what?"

I smirked, "You couldn't care less about hockey, could you?"

He just whistled lightly, "My dad talks about it all the time, so I just pick up on it here and there. Jenny is really into it with him, and they constantly fight about who's going to win the cup and everything. I just sit back and laugh."

I took a deep breath, well at least he wasn't a sports nut. I couldn't handle dating a sports nut. All they ever do is play sports with the boys, and if they aren't playing sports, they're talking about playing sports. It's nauseating really. I put the dishes in the rack and sighed. I guess this is over, now we have to go spend time with my family.

We walked into the living room, and the television was already on the sports channel. I didn't want to watch this, but I guess Morgan had already agreed. I doubt my father would be impressed if I bailed out now, so I took a seat in the chair by the fireplace while Morgan found a seat next to my father on the couch. The game started, and I just watched them, imagining this happening for years to come.

They were yelling profanities at the screen, yelling about some guy not defending properly. Then they were yelling about the goalie just letting pucks past him. It all seemed amusing, and if Morgan was pretending, he was doing an amazing job at acting. I sat with a book, reading while they watched the game.

"Well, that was one hell of a game! Do you think they'll make it into the playoffs?" My dad got up and stretched, he looked like he was ready for bed. "They almost make it every year, but then something goes wrong."

Morgan laughed, "They just need to keep their shit together."

"Well, thanks for coming over Morgan, I must retire."

And then my dad did something I'd never expect, he hugged Morgan goodbye.

Chapter Fourteen

I found the old yearbook from that year, and I laughed at everyone's pictures and how ludicrous everyone looked. We always tried to make everyone laugh, so I guess it worked out in the end. Then I saw the picture of Morgan and me in the "awards" section. That year had been a big turning point for the school. I took a deep breath as I read the letters underneath the picture, "Cutest Couple". It was something I never imagined true, so when the yearbook photographer took the picture, I assumed it was just for fun. Three months later when I got my yearbook, I had no words.

Morgan took it better than I did, as he flaunted that yearbook like it was the Holy Grail. He was extremely excited about being in it, especially since we got a little trophy. It was kind of amusing, even if some select people refused to believe we had won anything. As I looked over to the bookcase, seeing the trophy sitting on the shelf, I remembered that day like it was yesterday. The feelings all came crashing back inside me, and the pride was inevitable. We had won something most people would have killed to get.

"Awe! That is probably the best picture of you two I have ever seen! It looks so natural! I can't believe you won cutest couple, I'm kind of jealous." Jenny stifled a laugh as she closed her locker and put the yearbook in her other hand. She had been musing about this for hours now, but I didn't think it was that big of a deal. "I wonder if he's seen it yet, I'm sure he'll be super excited about it. I wish Julian and I could have won, I think we're adorable."

I laughed a little, trying to be as excited as her, "I don't think he'll care, it's just some stupid award we won at the high school. I bet he'll just shrug it off as coincidence."

As we made our way to math, at least fifteen people stopped me and congratulated me on the win. They awed and oohed about the picture and told me it was the best picture of all time. I didn't understand the whole spiel about it, but I just said thanks and continued on my way. The rest of my classes for the day seemed to fly by, and I really didn't like all the looks, but I guess it was for a good cause. At least it was civilized.

Lunch finally came around, and I was starving by the time it finally did. I grabbed my lunch and made my way to the table where everyone was sitting. Morgan didn't seem to be around, which made me kind of nervous since he was always here before I was. I sighed as I sat down, watching Jenny give Julian a peck on the lips, ew! Straight love was so gross.

After what seemed like hours, I looked around the cafeteria once more, but Morgan was nowhere to be seen. He had been absent the entire lunch, and I was not impressed. The least he could have done was text me that he wouldn't be here. Then I would have gone out with Kelly from my English class to lunch, but no, he didn't. So here I was, sitting in the cafeteria, watching Julian and Jenny undress and probably make love to each other with their eyes.

"Jenny, I'm going to go get some stuff from the car. Are you going to be able to maintain your dignity and not sleep with Julian right here in the middle of the cafeteria?"

As she gave me some sort of death glare, Jenny stuck up her middle finger, but her lips did not leave Julian's. Well, that's kind of awkward. I got up and walked out of the school, heading towards the cars. I was super excited my parents finally let me take a car for the day because it meant they were getting closer to trusting me to get my own car! Bus rides were not for this guy right here!

Opening the door, I searched for the sweater I needed to give back to Morgan. It had to be somewhere in here, I knew I got it this morning. I started rifling through everything. My dad really was a messy person, and he should probably clean out his car once in a while.

While searching for the sweater, I heard someone come up behind me. I turned around to see a smirking Morgan looking at me, his hands hidden behind his back, "Hey, Mattieboy."

I rolled my eyes, "Well, the mysterious Morgan creature finally appears. He's been vacant for a few hours now, especially through an awkward lunch where the Mattieboy species had to watch the Julian and Jenny creatures almost undress each other on the cafeteria table."

I felt his arms around me as I got out of the car, "Would the fact I was buying these make up for anything?"

I turned to look what he had bought, and I was astonished to see tickets to the latest Avril Lavigne concert. I couldn't hide the smile, "Where the hell did you get those? And flowers!" I looked at Morgan, who was obviously amused by my excitement.

"I had to go talk to one of my father's employees because they had extra tickets they were selling. I remembered you liked her, so we're going. The flowers are because we won Cutest Couple this year, and that kind of makes my life."

I giggled slightly, kissing Morgan lightly, "Well aren't you just the best boyfriend in the world."

He held his head up high, "Already knew that, Mattieboy."

An alarm on my phone went off, "Oh shit. I'm going to be late for English, and you know Mrs. P, she'll absolutely lose her mind if I'm late one more day. Are we hanging out after school?"

"Obviously."

I looked down at saw the sweater, "Here's your sweater."

He kissed me, "Looks better on you, you can have it."

Chapter Fifteen

*M*organ's mother was one in a million, and she liked the internet almost as much as her kids. Ask her about Facebook, and she knew the latest gossip. Ask her what an FML was, and she would be able to tell you the newest and latest fail the internet had to offer. She was so up to date with technology that she had the newest computer known to man, and every year, she got something different.

She didn't know what one acronym was, and one day she decided to ask her kids. I have never seen a more horrified look coming from my best friend, Jenny, than I did that day. She couldn't believe the words coming out of her mom's mouth, and all I could do was laugh. Mrs. Winters also had a sense of humor though, something I noticed Morgan got more than Jenny.

As we sat on the couch that day, we had a nice little conversation with Mrs. Winters about what exactly this acronym meant. I never really could forget the way she was so natural with everything, especially her beauty, and I guess that's where the MILF status came from.

The television droned on in the background of the living

room as we sat there talking about the upcoming graduation ceremony for Morgan and Julian. This year was a big year, and everyone wanted it to be the best thing of all time. The school had been around for one hundred years, a whole century. The school was taking it pretty seriously, so everything was being prepared a year before. Donations began pouring in sometime in September, and hundreds of thousands of dollars would be used this year.

"And a late cold front will be moving into the area, causing temperatures to drop dramatically over the next week. If you were starting to get out your summer clothes, I think now would be a good time to get your winter jacket back out," the weather woman droned on out of the speakers. I sighed as I turned to Morgan.

"It's supposed to get colder now! It's almost my birthday, and I won't be able to enjoy it. What the hell is up with that?" I pouted in the corner of the couch, convinced my birthday was going to be ruined.

Mrs. Winters walked into the room, twirling in the new dress she bought. "What do you guys think, does this scream cougar? I mean, I don't actually want to be a cougar, I just want people to think I look good enough to be one, or do I want to be a MILF? I hear that's a compliment."

Jenny started laughing, her eyes closing as tears slowly poured out, "MOM! Do you even know what that means? That is not something you really want to be labeled as." She wrinkled her nose, turning to Julian, "Do you think my mom is a MILF?"

Julian stuttered, spluttering some words here and there. I giggled as he struggled to find the right words, so I spoke up first, "Personally, I think your mom is totally a MILF. Maybe not for me personally, but I'm sure you could ask some of the guys at school, and they would agree with me."

Jenny looked horrified, "NO! That would be totally unnecessary. WHY WOULD YOU EVEN THINK

THAT!?"

"What does MILF stand for, Jenny?" Mrs. Winters looked amused, but she looked like she honestly did not know what it meant. She probably got the slang word from the internet. She twirled once more, "My boss' son says it's a compliment, not a lot of women get the status."

Before Jenny could interject, I looked at Mrs. Winters, "Well ma'am, it means *Mother I would Like to F-*" Jenny cut me off by pushing her hand onto my mouth. A glare coming from the small slits in her eyes warned me not to finish that sentence.

I didn't need to finish it before Mrs. Winters started laughing, "Oh, that's such a dirty little word, but I still think it's a compliment. Maybe I should pick you kids up from school tomorrow, so everyone can see me in my new dress. I like the status it would bring along."

Morgan started laughing, "If you showed up to pick your kids up in that, mother... you wouldn't get the MILF, you'd get the CMFM instead." He looked at me, a twinkle in his eyes, "And we really don't want my mom to get that label do we?"

I looked at Morgan with a slightly confused look, not knowing exactly where he was going with this. "What the hell is a CMFM?"

He just started laughing, smacking his knee, "You will find out later." Turning to his mother, "Are you going out tonight or something? Is that what the new dress is for?"

Mrs. Winters smiled, twirling one final time, "Actually, we are all going out. We have two special moments to celebrate. You all should go get dressed in the nicest clothes you have, we're going to the new restaurant on the east side."

"What are these special moments, Mrs. Winters?"

"The six-month anniversaries of your relationships. Both my kids have made it to six months, how exciting is that?

Hurry and go get ready."

Morgan got up, grabbing my hand, "Come on, Mattieboy, we've got some spiffing up to do." Pulling me upstairs, he closed the door as we entered the room. I was still a little astonished at the fact we had been dating for six months.

As I walked to the closet, Morgan pulled me into a hug and rested his chin on the top of my head, "Mattieboy, I love you. Are you still going to love me when I'm in college, and we see each other far less?"

I giggled, "Of course. Why would I stop loving you?"

He just pulled me in closer, I could feel something was wrong, but I couldn't put my finger on exactly what it was, "I'm just making sure, that's all."

Chapter Sixteen

*A*long with pictures, I found a smaller box in the corner. I picked it up and held it between my fingers. I knew Morgan was romantic, but that night when we were all around the table, he pulled out this small box and presented it to me. At first, I thought he was proposing, and I kind of freaked out. It had only been six months, and that seemed to be a little too soon to be thinking of marriage, but it turns out Morgan believed strongly in the idea of a promise ring.

So when he opened the box and took out the small diamond encrusted ring, I was having a mini panic attack. He was smiling the whole time, and he talked about us and the way he wanted us to be. It was at that moment, I realized Morgan was completely in love with me, and the thought of losing me when he went off to college really scared him. Here I was, thinking I was going to lose him to some of his college roommates, and it turns out he was thinking I'd find someone better at the school, maybe a freshman or something.

Every time I think of this day, I can't help but smile. I have never seen Morgan be so nervous about something, but this paved the road for *our relationship even further. I knew at this time I wanted to be with Morgan for longer than I had ever wanted to be with someone.*

We stepped into the restaurant, and the bright chandeliers gleamed with white light as we stepped past a birthday party. Images of important people through history lined the cream coloured walls. I stopped and looked at the painting of Julius Caesar, who had to be my all time favourite emperor of Rome. I was reading the little description when I felt a hand on the back of my shoulder, so I turned around to see Julian standing behind me.

"I took a whole class on Roman History, and it had to be the best class of my life. It was a really interesting culture." He looked upset about something, so I stood there for a second, pondering whether or not I should ask what was wrong.

After a few seconds, I decided Julian was not only my boyfriend's best friend, but my best friend's boyfriend, and if he was upset, I wanted to fix whatever it was. "Are you doing okay there Julian? You seem somewhat upset."

He looked down at the ground and then back up at me, before looking around the small room, "I'm just nervous. I graduate this year, and what if Jenny finds some other guy that spends more time with her, loves her more, or gets along better with her? I'm scared I'll get a call or something, and she'll be gone. What if I come back to visit, and she's moved on with some other guy? I don't think I could handle that; I love the little spitfire."

I sighed, why were both the men in my life having doubts? Were they both really this insecure? I put my hand on his shoulder, smiling up at him, "She loves you too. Have a little more faith in your relationship, I don't think Jenny is planning on letting go of you that quick. Plus, Morgan'll be going to the same school as you, so you'll at least be able to know what's going on at all times, right?"

Hanging his head down, Julian looked upset, "I guess

you're right. Do you like me? Will you make sure she doesn't move on?"

Before I could answer, Morgan slung his arm around my shoulders, "Our table is ready. Shall we go eat?"

I smiled at him, but looked at Julian, who I wanted so badly to make feel better, "Yea, let's go eat. I think we're all a bit hungry."

As we sat down at the table, Mrs. Winters smiled at all of us, she seemed to be glowing, maybe she was really excited that both her kids were seeing someone she actually liked. She reached into her purse and pulled out two envelopes, handing one to each of her kids. "This is for making a milestone in both your relationships. Six months may not seem like a big deal, but it's the little things that count the most. So here is a gift for the two of you. I hope you'll enjoy it as much as me and the mister think you will. Now, let's order and get this show on the road."

We were finishing up our desserts when Morgan stood up. His hands were shaking as he looked around the table, and I saw him take a deep breath as he turned to me. "I have an announcement to make. I wanted to do this in private, but I am so excited about this I don't think I can hold it in anymore." He turned to me, reached into his pocket, and pulled out a box. I started to breathe heavy. What was he doing? "Mattieboy, when we first met, I knew you were the one. I felt something inside me, so I have decided to give you this." He opened the box to show a ring with a single diamond in the middle and a white gold band hugging it tightly. "I'm giving you a promise ring, so even when I'm in college, and we're miles apart, you'll remember that I will always be with you. Then one day, we'll get married."

I started to cry; the gesture he was doing was so beautiful. Not to mention the ring looked expensive and unique. "Morgan! I wasn't prepared. This is so exciting!"

He put the ring on my finger, pulling me into a hug, "I

hope you'll love me for as long as I'll love you."

I choked back tears, "Of course I will."

Mrs. Winters stood up, "Awe! Congratulations you guys. I'm so happy for you. I also have an announcement, and I have to say it now, it's good news." She gleamed with pride, looking at us, "I'm pregnant!"

Chapter Seventeen

*A*fter the news coming from Mrs. Winters, I learned some things about Morgan that I didn't know before. They say it takes a lifetime to know a person, and I would have to agree. I had known Morgan for six months and yet, here I was sitting watching him talk about how awesome it would be to have a smaller sibling to take care of. His eyes were sparkling whenever he talked about being there for his brother or sister. It was at that moment I realized that Morgan would really have liked to be a father. We never talked about a family, seeing as it was so early in our relationship. I just assumed he didn't want children, knowing full well a lot of gay families were not popping up everywhere, but I was wrong.

That weekend, we made a trip up to the cottage that the Winters owned, and I found a new respect for Morgan. His younger cousin was there and at that moment, I saw how good he was with kids. The glimmer in his eye as he played around with his cousin really made me see what kind of father Morgan would turn out to be. I knew I wanted to be an amazing father, just like Morgan, but I was also terrified of *turning out like my own father. Even if he said he loved me, I knew deep down inside he was disappointed in my life. I didn't want that for my child.*

"So, Mr. and Mrs. Winters, have you guys decided on a name for the baby? I know it might be early on, but everyone wants the perfect name, no?" Julian was leaning in his seat, trying to get as close to them as possible.

I shifted uncomfortably in my seat. I hated long car rides, but I said I would go to the cottage with Morgan. I needed a break anyways. The trees rolled by as we drove down the highway. My butt was becoming numb, and I felt like we had been sitting here for hours. I kept looking at the clock, realizing it had only been an hour.

"We haven't completely decided yet, but I think we're looking at Kyler for a boy and Karen for a girl. Who knows, maybe we'll just name them Mattie." Mr. Winters winked through the rear-view mirror at me, I turned my head and laughed lightly.

"I don't think that would be a good idea. I don't think I could handle dating a Mattie and then having a brother named Mattie. That would be awkward if we were ever in bed and I was..." Morgan started talking, and my eyes bugged out of my head as I smacked him on the arm, signalling for him to stop talking "... I just think it would be weird to have two Matties in my life."

Jenny started giggling, turning her head towards me, "What do you think, Mattie? Is there a name you'd like for your future kid? I know Morgan already has his picked out." Jenny threw her hands up, "Not that they were very original, what kind of original names are Karen and Benjamin?"

I laughed, shaking my head at the names. "They're cute!"

"Oh, just so you kids know, my sister will be there." Mrs. Winters was looking at her phone, "She just texted me that she was able to get the weekend off from work. Mattie, you'll love Stella, she is honestly one of the best people I know."

Morgan looked like he was getting excited, "Is Kendall going to be there as well!?"

Mrs. Winters was nodding, "Absolutely. We haven't seen that little spitfire in a few months, I know he is super excited to see you Morgan. Apparently he kept asking Stella if he was going to see you. He says that your tickles are the best in the business."

Morgan proudly smiled, "Of course they are, I'm just awesome like that."

I sighed. I felt like the outsider here. Everyone else had met these people, and I was new. What if this Kendall didn't like me? What if he thought I was taking Morgan away from him? Did he even know what being gay was?

The car came to a stop in front of a huge looking house. Where the hell were we? "Is this..."

Morgan slapped my back, "This is the best place in the world. It's like living at a home away from home."

As I walked into the building, I noticed it looked like the Winters' house back in town, which made me confused. I thought we were camping? I looked around the main room, seeing all the bedrooms. Morgan grabbed my hand and pulled me into a room, closing the door.

"What are you doing, Morgan? I was trying to look over the house."

Morgan pushed me onto the bed, "Want to make a family of our own, Baby?" He was smirking, and I started giggling, "Come on Mattie, we'll have beautiful children."

"And who is getting pregnant, because I'm pretty sure we both are missing a few important parts, such as a uterus."

Morgan started laughing, getting off the bed after kissing me lightly, "I guess there is the case of the missing uterus." He opened the door, motioning for me to follow, "I'll take you to my favourite place in the entire cottage. I used to go there to read and take a breather from all the children of the family. It's beautiful, follow me."

I followed Morgan to the rooftop, where they had a patio set. I couldn't believe the view of the lake and other cottages lining the woods around us. "This is beautiful."

My thoughts were interrupted as a woman walked out with a child, "UNCLE MORGGIE!"

The child wrapped his arms around Morgan, a huge smile on his face. I turned to say hi to the woman, but my mouth dropped open. "Mrs. Daniels?"

She looked at me, tensing up immediately, "Oh... Hi Mattie. What are you doing here?"

I stuttered, "What are you doing here, actually?"

Chapter Eighteen

A few years before this fateful day of meeting Morgan's aunt, my father had an... indiscretion with his secretary. My mother totally forgave the accident, but my father had to send a cheque to someone in a different town for what he called "an oopsie". Staring at Mrs. Daniel's eyes, I realized exactly what had happened. My father had a child with this woman, who turned out to be Morgan's aunt. Well, this wasn't something I was totally prepared for. I should have known when the name Stella came up, I remembered my mother yelling her name over and over.

I was visibly tense, and Morgan could sense it. I have never in my life known a moment like this would happen. It turns out Mrs. Daniel's just told everyone her actual husband got her pregnant, but Kendall looked a lot like my father and not so much like her husband. I took a deep breath and calmed myself, trying to figure out exactly what I was going to do. Should I tell Morgan what happened or should I stay back and keep her secret safe?

"Do you two know each other?" Morgan made a face,

looking back from me to her. He was standing beside me, "Aunt Stella, how do you know Mattie?"

She smiled slightly, "I was about to ask you the same thing, Morgan. How do you know Mattie?"

I realized she was avoiding the question to try and think of something to say. I felt bad for her, but I knew if this little secret of hers got out this weekend, it would be ruined. What about Morgan and I? How would he handle the situation?

"He's my boyfriend, actually, but that still doesn't answer my question. How do you guys know each other?" Morgan was tense, and I could actually feel just how much when he gripped my shoulder, waiting for one of us to answer. I only knew that Stella was my dad's secretary, but that would turn into an even more awkward conversation.

"He was in my piano class for a year, but he didn't want to stick with it. Apparently the piano is not for Mattie." She seemed so cool and collected, and Morgan turned to me and smiled.

"Is this true? You don't like the piano?"

"I tried, but I just failed. I skipped out on a few of her classes. I'm sorry, I didn't expect her to be your aunt." I saw him visibly relax. I took a deep breath as I tried hard to conceal the anger running through me.

"Well, I guess this makes it less awkward. I didn't think Mattie would know you, so he's not an outsider anymore. This is my cousin, Kendall. He's only the most perfect child."

Kendall seemed distracted as he waved at me, "Morggie! Can we go to the beach, I made something last night for you when I was here but mommy wouldn't let me bring it back. Come! Let's go look at it." The little boy started pulling his hand, "This way!"

Morgan smiled, "I'll be back." He moved from the rooftop as Kendall pulled him down the stairs.

I stood there awkwardly while Stella looked me up and down, "I see you've grown up quite a lot, Mattie."

I looked over at her, and she now looked slightly older than a few minutes ago, "I won't say anything, you can take a deep breath. I really don't know how Morgan would take the news that my father had an affair with you. It would probably destroy any image he has of the both of us. I need you to keep your cool and pretend none of that happened." I can't believe how in charge I sounded. My voice was a little shaky, but I couldn't let Morgan find out the truth.

"Good. We'll pretend you were one of my students. That's all. Now, I need to go help my sister unpack since she's pregnant and all." Walking away, I felt the air around me become much less tense. This was going to be an extremely awkward weekend if she was here the whole time.

I walked down the stairs to the living room to see Jenny and Julian sitting on the couch with Monopoly opened and ready to go. Jenny smiled up at me and motioned for me to come over, "Hey! Wanna play a round? I'm the best in the world, so if you're intimidated, please just step away."

I laughed, "I never lose." I sat down on the floor, looking at the both of them, "Let's do this."

A few hours later, Morgan walked back into the cottage with Kendall right on his heels. He looked at us and smiled, "Who's winning?"

Jenny huffed, "That little..." She caught herself about to swear, calming herself slightly, "Mattie is winning, and he owns 90% of the board. Julian just went bankrupt, and I'm pretty sure in a few moves I will be too. I didn't know your boyfriend was such a good monopolist!"

I just smirked at her as Morgan sat down next to me, "Kendall wants to ask you something. He's kind of nervous though." He pointed to Kendall, who was sitting at the kitchen table, pulling out a puzzle. "Kendall, you can ask him now. He's listening."

The small boy looked down at the ground, fiddling with his thumbs, "I was wondering if you'd make a puzzle with me. Morgan always gets the pieces out of order, so I was hoping you could do better."

I smiled, "Absolutely." I looked at Jenny, "I guess you win by default. I have to forfeit because a four-year-old needs my attention."

Jenny smiled, "I will keep this board open, we're finishing this off, Mattie."

I walked over to the table with Kendall and started putting puzzle pieces together, trying to see how everything fit. Kendall looked at me and smiled, "I like you, Mattie. You better keep my Morggie happy."

I ruffled his hair, "I would love to, Kendall."

Chapter Nineteen

*M*organ *took a picture of Kendall and I playing with the puzzle, and every time I look at it I start to laugh. I seemed to replace Morgan for a few short hours, and Kendall wanted me to make another puzzle over and over again. I just kept making puzzles. He seemed to take a liking to me. I was surprised by the four-year-old's attentive nature to the situation at hand, but I guess when you're that young, you don't care about labels. You just want people to be happy and enjoy each other's company. He didn't think of Morgan as his "gay" uncle. It was refreshing to hear such maturity from such a young person.*

As we finished off another puzzle, Mrs. Winters called us all to come out for dinner. They had made a fire and were now roasting hot dogs. I climbed out of the chair and was followed closely by Kendall, who seemed to want to spend every minute with me. Morgan gave me a quick smirk since he was free from the shackles of the small child. I just stuck my tongue out at him and walked out into the backyard. I sat down and without even a second of thought, Kendall sat down right next to me.

"Will you make me a hot dog, Uncle Mattie?" Staring up at me with wide eyes, I couldn't help but laugh. Not only had I become his next best friend, but he also decided I was good enough to be considered an uncle.

"Sure, buddy, can you go get me two hot dogs. I'm starving, so I need to eat too."

He got up and skipped over to the table, grabbing what he needed. I felt someone sit beside me, wrapping familiar arms around me, "He seems to like you. I see you're also wonderful with kids."

I smacked Morgan's leg, "Don't even think about it. You cannot impregnate me!" I giggled as Morgan gave me puppy eyes, "I'm not ready for that, a child of my own. I can give this one as much candy as I want and in the end, I can just pawn him back to his parents."

Morgan laughed as he watched me roasting the hot dogs, with his head leaning on my shoulder. Listening to the conversation, I was content with the current situation, even if that woman was sitting across the fire from me. I could feel her eyes staring at me as if I was going to say something.

"Are they ready, I am hungry. Oh, so hungry," Kendall was whining, I looked down at him and smiled.

"Do you want some bug crawling in your tummy?"

His eyes got the size of saucers, "What? No! Bugs don't crawl in my stomach!"

"If you eat this without cooking it right, you will. Just wait a few more minutes, and then you can eat all the hot dogs you want." I tried to hold back my laughter, but Morgan was already holding his gut at our conversation.

Kendall sat beside me intently watching me cook his dinner, never taking his eyes off the sparkling mess the juice from the hot dog made as it hit the fire below. After a few minutes, I grabbed a hot dog bun and put it inside, giving it to Kendall.

"There you go, buddy, eat up."

He quickly scrambled to the picnic table to get condiments, and in his absence Morgan sat beside me, resting his head back on my shoulder, "Why are you so good with kids?"

I smirked down at him, "I don't know, maybe because sometimes I feel I may be dating one."

With a quick flick of his wrist, Morgan slapped me. "Mattieboy! I am not a child. I don't even act like one!" His lip quivered slightly as he looked up at me with puppy dog eyes. I couldn't even hold my laughter in as he looked at me because he was acting like a child right now.

I looked to the other side of me after a few seconds, and Kendall had found a comfortable position next to me. His little hands were eagerly wrapped around his food as he devoured the hot dog. Relish and ketchup blotted the plate he had, and his mouth was full of the evidence. He was just smiling down at his food, content that he was eating something I had cooked him. It was adorable, I felt a satisfaction running through me.

"How's the food, Kendall?"

He just smiled, looking up at me and nodding. It was adorable.

The fire crackled on as we sat in silence, watching the embers fly into the sky. It was getting late, so I decided to call it a night. Kendall was right behind me followed by Morgan. Looking at me with the same puppy eyes Morgan liked to use, Kendall started to whimper, "Can I sleep with you tonight, Mattie?"

Patting his head, "You have to share a room with your mommy, but I'll see you bright and early tomorrow, I promise okay?"

Giving me a sad look, he sighed, "Okay. I'll see you tomorrow morning. Goodnight, Mattie." After a quick and unexpected hug, Kendall bounced off into the room across the cottage from us. Walking inside the room, Morgan just smiled as he pushed me against the wall.

"I never thought we would be alone." His hands ran through my hair as his lips brushed against mine. Shutting the door with my foot, I took the initiative to push him onto the bed and crawl on top of him, throwing my shirt to the floor.

"I guess we should make use of this room we have alone, shouldn't we?"

Smirking, Morgan threw his shirt beside mine, "I think that would be a wise idea."

I brought my lips down to Morgan's, pressing them down hard as the passion leaking from our pores fueled our every move. I loved feeling him kissing me back, showing me he loved me with everything he had. We listened to the fire crackling outside as we made love that night.

Chapter Twenty

I found a picture of Morgan and I sitting on a towel at the beach, the sun glaring down on our skin. I had been with him for almost seven months, and not one time had he ever gotten jealous of my closeness with anyone back home. This day was different. Maybe it was because nobody had paid particular attention to me back at school, but that day, a guy was flirting with me as I tanned. Morgan had been playing with Kendall in the water, and as he started moving towards us, I could see something lingering in his blue eyes. I had never seen him green with jealousy before until that moment.

He stood beside us, talking to the guy about what he was doing. When the guy talked about thinking I was cute and wondering if he was my older brother, Morgan gave him a death glare as he told him we were dating. The guy left and apologized, but Morgan just stared him down, watching him reunite with his friends down the beach. As he lay down next to me, wrapping an arm protectively around my waist, I couldn't help but feel proud that Morgan would get jealous over someone. For the first time in my life, I actually felt wanted.

The sun was shining down on me as I lay, sprawled out on the beach towel. It's rays were welcomed and maybe I could give myself a slight tan before summer was over. I just wanted to be a darker shade of pale. As I lay on the beach towel, I felt a shadow blocking out my sun, and l look up expecting to see Morgan. I was caught off guard when a young man stood smiling down at me instead. I just smiled back, wondering what he was doing.

"Hey there, cutie. My name's Jason, what's yours?"

I just continued to look up at him, oblivious to his advances, "I'm Mattie."

Sitting next to me, this Jason kid kept talking, I was just trying to get a tan, "Do you have a cottage up here? My family owns one across the lake, but this beach is much better than ours, so we just swim over here. I hate seaweed, and the people over here make sure there is none in the water. How old are you? You look like you're still in high school. I'm twenty-one."

I was trying to ignore him, but he didn't seem to get the drift. Where was Morgan when you needed him?

"Are you the silent type? Don't be nervous, I'm just super excited to see another cute guy around here. I mean, unless you're straight then that would be super awkward. Are you straight?"

Before I could answer, I felt another shadow looming over me. I sighed as I looked up, expecting one of this guy's friends to come and try and have a conversation. Instead, I looked into the eyes of an extremely pissed off Morgan. I took a deep breath, smiling at him.

"Oh hey, Babe. Done with the kid already? I hope you wore him out, I don't think I can handle another night of puzzles."

"Who's this?" He didn't even respond to my question. Was it sick of me to think he was cute when he was jealous?

"Hi! My name's Jason and you are?" Standing up, Jason

was actually a lot shorter than I had noticed, standing a whole foot below Morgan. I could tell he was double thinking his decision to talk to me now with my boyfriend towering over him.

"I'm Morgan and this is my boyfriend. Are you a friend of his?" He already knew the answer to his question, but I guess he wanted to confirm it. Maybe this guy was a long lost friend or something.

"No, I was just striking up a conversation with someone I saw, but I see I made a mistake, so I'm going to find my friends and maybe go for a fire. Sorry to bother you. Goodbye." Walking off quickly and tripping over the sand, Jason moved back to his friends.

I was internally laughing as I looked up at Morgan, "Hello, jealous monster."

Lying down next to me, Morgan wrapped a protective arm around my waist as he sighed; "I'm sorry, I just knew he was up to no good. I used to go to school with him before he transferred to the private sector. He's used to getting everything he wants, and I knew by the look in his eye he wanted you."

I just started laughing, and I don't really know why. Maybe it was the fact Morgan was getting so defensive about me or maybe it was the look he was giving me when telling his little story. I didn't know, all I knew is that it was hilarious.

"Seriously, Morgan? You think I'm going to leave you for a prep school jerk who probably would use me and move on?" I continued to laugh, trying to speak at the same time, "M-morgan... you... are..."

I didn't get to finish my sentence as Morgan pulled my head into his hands and kissed me gently on the lips. "Just shut up, please." I was still mentally laughing, even as he kissed me on the beach.

A few hours later we were packing up our things when

deep dark clouds rolled in from the east side of the beach, bringing with it a whole bunch of rain and thunder. We ran screaming like little children to the cottage, running inside laughing as we dried ourselves off.

"Hey, Mattieboy, wanna try another game of monopoly?" Morgan smirked as he pulled out the board game, and I knew exactly where this was going. "It'll be fun, maybe I can be the banker this time."

Julian swiped the box out of Morgan's hands, "No! For some reason, every time we play you always seem to magically have more fifty thousand dollar bills than the rest of us. I think your mother will be the banker."

We played board games for a few hours until Morgan fell asleep with his head on my shoulder.

Chapter Twenty-One

*M*ay turned into June, and June ended earlier than I would have expected it to. As we stood in front of the school for prom, it started slowly hitting me that school was almost over, and Morgan would be leaving for college. He would be gone from the school and my life for most of the year. I didn't really want to think about it, but he seemed to think nothing would change. I think part of him was naive, and part of him just didn't want anything to change. That night we hung out with all his friends and some of the people in my class who were dating seniors.

It was also the night we had our first slow dance. As we swayed to the music, I looked up at Morgan, and for the first time in our entire relationship, I decided right then and there he was the one for me. We may have only been dating for eight months, but that very night when he asked me the question I did not expect, I had to say something positive. After a few deep breaths, I finally decided to answer him the only way I thought acceptable.

The sounds from the speakers hit the walls and bounced

back into my ears. I had been sitting at the table for a few minutes, watching everyone get drunk or dance the night away. I felt lethargic because I had eaten way too much food, but the buffet had been calling my name all night. So I finally dragged my body over and filled two plates, before wobbling back to the table. I felt someone's hand on my back as I dug into the Chinese food in front of me with rice slowly falling out of my mouth. God, how attractive I must have looked right then.

"Hungry are we, Mattie?" Julian sat down beside me, stole a spring roll from my plate and shoved it in his mouth, making his cheeks pop out like that of a squirrel. He slowly started to chew as he drank from the red glass sitting on the table. "I haven't seen you out on the dance floor yet, and where the hell is Morgan? I haven't seen him all night."

I just nibbled on the rice and shrugged. I had seen him before we got here, but he seemed to vanish before we even had a chance to eat. I wasn't worried because he was probably doing something with his art teacher, who wanted him to be his teacher's aid next year. I guess Mr. Canders saw the hurt in my eyes when I told him Morgan would be leaving next year, and he wanted him to stay with me. A sweet thought if you really ask me.

"What the hell are you party bums doing? Eating again, Mattie! You've had like seven plates of rice. Where the hell are you storing all that food?" Jenny sat down on Julian's lap, stealing yet another spring roll from my plate. I growled as she shoved it in her mouth, but she just smiled as she chewed on what was supposed to be mine.

Julian kissed Jenny's cheek, standing up and carrying her bridal style towards the dance floor, "We'll be over here if you need us, Mattie. I think it's time Jenny and I get our groove on, if you know what I mean." A sly wink left Julian's eyes, and I rolled my own. Jenny smacked him on the shoulder and yelled something about personal business.

A few moments after they departed, I was finishing up the third plate of rice when I felt someone wrap their arms around my neck. I knew it was Morgan from the smell of his cologne and the feel of his touch as he began trailing kisses up the side of my neck. "Sorry I've been away, I was helping the teacher with a project. Do you want to dance? We still haven't had our first slow dance yet."

I smiled, grabbing a glass of water and letting the cool liquid wash the rice down my throat, "I guess you're right. I would like to dance with you." Taking my hand in his, Morgan lead me out to the dance floor. A slow song came over the speakers as he pulled my arms onto his shoulders and then wrapped his arms around my waist.

We swayed to the music with my head leaning on his chest. I could feel people watching us, but I really didn't care. I just wanted to feel close to him before it was all over. He would be leaving in a couple of months, and this would be one of the last times I would be able to feel him close enough to hear his breathing.

The music went on as other couples joined in on the dancing, each of us staying close enough to our lovers we had no worry of smacking into each other. I could feel Morgan's heart pounding louder than usual, and I could feel the sweat beading off his forehead. I looked up at him, seeing the worry in his eyes about something.

"Is everything okay? You seem a bit off today." His brown eyes darted around the room, his breaths becoming more and more rapid. I was starting to worry when he broke off with me, looking around the room for what seemed like an escape.

"There's something I've got to ask you, Mattieboy. I know this seems rushed and sudden, but I really need to get an answer from you." He looked down at me, worry starting to come out from my deep subconscious.

"Sure, you can ask me anything, you know that. What

seems to be going on?" My mind was racing a million miles a minute, and I was worried he had done something absolutely horrible. He reached into his pocket, bringing out something in his hand.

I would never have expected what happened next. Morgan got down on one knee in the middle of the dance floor, opening a small box. "Mattieboy, I just wanted to ask you if you would marry me?"

Chapter Twenty-Two

The ring shone throughout the entire dance floor, and as I stared at it sitting in the box, I couldn't help but feel a surge of happiness flowing throughout my body. I hadn't expected anything of this relationship at the beginning, but with seven months behind us, I could see for sure that this was something that was going to last an extremely long time. I couldn't help the happiness I felt that night, a stupid smirk starting to grow on my lips as he knelt on the ground, holding the small box up to my face.

I could see Jenny from the corner of my eye smirking at me, as if she knew exactly what was going to happen. I had gone from being concerned with the small things to being overwhelmed by the fact that the boy I wanted to spend the rest of my life with wanted to spend his life with me as well. The satisfaction was running rampant throughout my brain, and all I could think about was how surprised my parents would be at the news. Taking a deep breath that night, I thought about everything that I could say, but I knew exactly what I should say to him.

My hands were trembling, and I watched his movements as he knelt down on the floor. His words resonated through my ears. Had I actually heard him right? Did he seriously just ask me to marry him? Me, Mattie Hawkins was being proposed to by THE Morgan Winters? I pinched myself lightly to see if I was sleeping, but the skin turned red, and it hurt a little, signalling I was awake, and this was really happening.

I could see Jenny on the sidelines, holding onto Julian as she smirked in our direction. I bet she knew this was going to happen all night. What a night to propose to someone - the night of your senior prom. Taking a few slightly deep breaths, I looked back down at Morgan, light flashing in his eyes showing off the worry that started to settle inside them.

I didn't realize I had been standing here for five minutes not answering him. I smiled down at him, holding out my hand, "Do you even need to ask? Of course I will. I would love to be Mattie Winters."

Warm arms wrapped around my small body as Morgan pulled me into his embrace, his musky odor catching itself in my nostrils. I could hear him crying. I hope they were tears of happiness, and he hadn't been hoping I would reject him.

"Are you okay, Morgan?"

He sniffled slightly, pulling me in closer, "I couldn't be happier. I honestly was starting to lose hope in love, but then you came along and changed everything. I put on a show, pretending I knew what was going to happen, but I was so in love with you that very moment our hands touched at the school. I wouldn't want to be with anyone else."

I wanted to start crying myself, but I kept my composure. I felt someone's hands wrap themselves around my other side. I smelt her perfume enveloping me, and I smiled. I turned my body slightly to see Jenny hugging me, Julian right behind her.

"Congratulations, Mattie. I'm so excited you're going to be my brother-in-law!"

Julian was smiling at Morgan, "I'm so glad you found someone, Morgan. I was starting to worry about you. Congratulations, buddy."

Morgan broke away from the hug, taking my hand and pushing me onto the dance floor, "I love you, Mattieboy."

I smashed my head into his chest, "I love you too, Morgan."

The sounds of the music seemed to drown out as I realized what was really happening. My thoughts had become a broken up, jumbled mess in my head. I didn't know who I should tell. I didn't know if my parents should know. Do we keep this a secret from them? My mind was racing a million miles per minute when someone over the loudspeaker interrupted the moment.

"Students, if you wouldn't mind taking a seat at your tables. It's time to release the names of this year's Prom King and Queen. This is an exciting year for the school, and those named this year's royalty will go down in history. It's been a hundred years since we opened the doors, and I am so excited to announce this."

Everyone took their seats, and giggling commenced as all the students found their tables. I was too excited to sit down, but with the disapproving looks coming from the teachers, I decided it was a good idea just to sit down and calm down. I sat next to Morgan, just as the loudspeaker came to life again, and the principal of our school opened an envelope.

"To all those on the ballot, even though I know it is an honour to be royalty, please remember you are all kings and queens in your own rank. We have given ballots to absolutely every single person in the school, and these two students won by a landslide. Without further ado, I will now announce this year's KING and QUEEN!"

A few moments and many shuffles of paper later, she

finished opening the envelope in her hands. Clearing her throat, a stunned look came onto her face as she searched the room, "Well... this is a first for the school. How exciting is this? I actually can't believe this is happening; we'll be on the news for this." A few moments of quiet, and finally she looked back at the school, "Sorry, this is a proud moment for all of us. I'm so glad this is happening."

A few murmurs went around the room. Why was she taking so long to announce this? I was sure it was going to be Clarabelle and Markus; the two of them were just the cutest couple of all time.

One more look around the room and she cleared her throat once more, "The king and queen for this year are..."

Chapter Twenty-Three

*L*ooking over at the bookcase in the left corner of the living room, I smiled as I looked at both the crowns sitting on the shelf. It had been a great victory for both Morgan and myself, and something we never would have thought possible. In all the years of the school being open, not once had a gay couple been nominated, let alone won the title of Prom King and King. The gold on the crowns had slightly worn away after all these years, but the memories associated with them were something you could never have taken away.

After the prom, the four of us decided to head over to Denny's for a very late night breakfast. It was Morgan's favourite meal of the day, and he could have eaten pancakes and eggs every meal for at least the next ten years. I loved it too, but he just seemed to always be eating something associated with breakfast. As we sat in the booth, Jenny and I talked about our plans for next year, and Morgan and Julian talked about all the amazing things they were going to do in college. I had never seen Morgan so excited, which actually upset me a little. How could he be so excited knowing he would be gone from my life for most *of the year?*

"You must be living on a high note right now, hey, Mattieboy?" Jenny smirked as she flung a piece of egg at me.

I squealed as I moved my head, making the egg hit the back of my seat. I stuck my tongue out at Jenny as I prepared a spoonful of oatmeal for her, "I'm amazed we even won. I thought for sure some of the other couples would have won because they all seemed so adorable."

Wrapping his arm around my shoulders, Morgan gave me a look, " Obviously we are the cutest of them all. I mean, with a boyfriend like you, who wouldn't vote for us."

Jenny put up her arm, and she was met with the spoonful of oatmeal to her chest. She shrieked a little and hid her face in Julian's shoulder, as she pouted slightly at my accomplishment. I just shrugged and continued to eat away as if nothing had happened.

"I can't wait until mom sees this. She'll be absolutely elated we won. She was Prom Queen back in her heyday too. I forgot to show you the pictures in her yearbook. She's probably just going to smile and nod her head since she knew one of us would win anyways." Morgan finished his eggs and pushed the plate to the side of the table.

"Too bad it wasn't with Dad. That would have been even better, but I guess they didn't know each other until college." Jenny was diving into her pancakes, and I gave her a horrified look as she devoured every last bit.

A few moments later the waitress came to the table, a huge smile on her face, "So I was talking to my manager, who has been married to his husband for three years, and he noticed the crowns. He bought you guys some cake for the occasion. Did you just win the crown tonight?"

Morgan smiled up at her with an arm slung around my shoulders, "Yessery! Mattieboy and I just won Prom King and King. It's a pretty glorious moment, I must say."

The waitress giggled, putting the cake on the table, "Well,

congratulations. I'm so glad to see the world progressing just a little bit. I hope you enjoy the win, I know it must have been a pretty amazing feeling."

Suddenly feeling everyone's eyes on me, I slouched down in my seat, turning seventy shades of red, "Thank you. We'll enjoy this. Thank your manager as well, I'm sure going to enjoy getting fat off this."

She just giggled again, walking away with the empty plates. I looked down at the cake and shot a glare at Jenny, "Now, this is my cake, not yours. So you just take that fork and shove it somewhere else."

Jenny gave me a slightly hurt look but drove her fork into the cake, and she just started to eat, "Wait, what were you saying? I couldn't hear you over the sound of the cake telling me to eat it."

Laughing, I started to help with the cake, eating every last bit of it. When we were finished, we paid our bill and headed out into the cool summer night. Morgan grabbed my hand as we walked, a smirk on his face. I just reveled in the moment, knowing that soon he would be gone, and I wouldn't be able to do this anymore.

When we got back to the Winters' house, everyone flung themselves on the nearest couches. We were all exhausted and full from our meal. Mrs. Winters and Mr. Winters were outside having some champagne, and they yelled at us to come outside. Reluctantly, we all got up and made our way outside. Sitting on the patio, we all looked at the beautiful night sky.

"I hear congratulations are in order, boys. Jenny texted me earlier to tell me you won Prom King and King." Mrs. Winters was glowing, obviously excited about the situation.

"That's pretty exciting, your mother and I won the titles as well, although we were at totally different schools at the time." Mr. Winters smiled at us, his champagne glass shining in the fire they had going.

"It is pretty exciting if you ask me, I can't wait to show my parents, they will be so gosh darn excited."

We all quit talking and just watched the stars, Morgan nuzzled his face into my shoulder. I could feel the smile on his face, and I could tell exactly what he was thinking. "We're going to go to bed, we'll see you all tomorrow." With a few good-nights and whatnot, we made our way to his room.

Shutting the door and pushing me to the bed, Morgan smiled, "Have I told you I love you."

Chapter Twenty-Four

I remembered Morgan's heartbeat the most because of the way it never stayed the same. Sometimes it was very fast, and sometimes it was very slow. I thought it was because he was nervous or something. The first time I noticed this, we were laying in the grass in the field behind the school watching the stars together. My head was on his chest, and I was listening to the thumping. I didn't think anything of it, I honestly thought it was completely normal.

Then the news hit that Morgan had an arrhythmia, a condition of the heart that gave him his irregular heartbeats. He was diagnosed a few months after prom, and the doctors gave him only a year or so to live, if even that. I have never felt my life being crushed as I did at that moment. I didn't know what to do or what to think. I just wanted everything to be okay. In the good old Morgan fashion, he kept telling me it had been like that for years, and nothing had ever happened. He said I had nothing to worry about. I believed him at first, but I was so wrong to think nothing would ever happen to the man I loved.

The air outside was a little bit chilly, and the wind was

picking up but I was comfortable sitting in the grass with Morgan. My head rested on his chest, and his arms wrapped around me, making the heat from his body seep into my own. A small smile was on my face as he pointed out some of the constellations in the sky. I never really paid attention in science class, but when Morgan talked all I could do was listen.

The silence gave me time to think as well about everything that was currently going on. A few months ago I was alone, wondering if I would ever find someone who would love me and now here I was, wrapped in the arms of someone who would soon be called my husband. My thoughts kept wrapping themselves around that word, *husband*.

"You're awfully quiet there, Mattieboy. What are you thinking about?" Morgan looked down at me with a small frown starting to form on his lips.

I pushed myself closer into his arms, pressing my cheek against his neck, "Nothing at all. I was just thinking about what is happening. Did you ever think you would be getting married this soon?"

A contented sigh left Morgan's lips, "I didn't think I would ever be this happy. Honestly, it's been so long since I felt content being with someone. That day before we ran into each other, I was so confused with someone else I thought I wanted to be my boyfriend, but as soon as I saw you, everything became clear. Everything just seemed to make sense at that very moment. I don't think I could imagine my life without you now."

Just the answer I was looking for. I kissed him softly, letting my lips linger on his for a few seconds, a smile breaking through. "You're such a dweeb."

He ruffled my hair as I lied back down on his chest, listening to the slow beat of his heart. Everything seemed so right at the moment, and I don't think I would have changed anything. As I started to fall asleep on him, he quickly picked me up and walked me to the car, put me in the passenger seat, and started driving to his house.

I had pretty much moved in with the Winters, and I had only been home once or twice this month. Surprisingly, my parents were totally cool with everything. They even praised me for finding someone as amazing as Morgan. As our parents made preparations for the wedding, Morgan and I just took our time falling more in love with each other.

I was startled awake when the car suddenly jerked to the side of the road and stopped. My eyes shot open, and I looked over at Morgan, who was turning a light shade of white as his face contorted in a confused expression. Suddenly I started to panic, when I realized he was holding his chest.

"What the hell is happening? Morgan, are you okay? Morgan!?" He was silent, with his face finally resting on the steering wheel. I couldn't see his chest moving anymore proving he wasn't getting any air into his lungs. I grabbed my phone, unlocked the screen, before calling the ambulance. I kept shaking him, screaming something incoherent throughout the car.

It took fifteen minutes for the ambulance to arrive there, but it felt more like a year with the way I was panicking. I ran out of the car to flag the ambulance down. I could see Morgan struggling to breathe, but he was still alive. His mother had warned me about the condition he had a few months back, but he had been doing fine. Now all of a sudden everything was happening at once.

The paramedic pulled Morgan out of the car and placed him on the ground. He ripped open his shirt, and placed the defibrillator on his heart. I could hear them yelling their medical terms. I could hear the sound of the electric shock, but I couldn't go around the other side of the car to look. I couldn't look at him lying there helplessly without life in his body.

The last thing I remembered seeing was Morgan being lifted into the ambulance on a stretcher as the lights flashed maniacally at me. I remember hearing the paramedic yelling at me, "Are you coming with us? Hey, Mister! Are you coming with us or not? We have to go now."

I was in shock as I ran to the back of the ambulance. I threw myself into the back and gripped Morgan's hands. The door closed, and we started rushing off to the hospital. I was crying, and tears were soaking my face along with the shirt I was wearing.

I just sat there, quietly calling out his name and telling him to stay with me.

Chapter Twenty-Five

*A*s I sat looking at all the pictures strewn around the room, I couldn't help but let out a small sigh along with a few tears that spilled out of my eyes. I had been staring at his pictures for hours now, wondering if this was really happening or if it was all just a dream, and soon I would wake up and everything would be back to normal. I started collecting the pictures into the shoebox again, making sure to pack them as nicely as possible. I would have to look at them again sometimes if I wanted to remember what we had.

The bells at the church started to ring, signalling it was about to start. I put the shoebox back on the shelf and adjusted my tuxedo, making sure the wrinkles that had formed were gone, and the shirt underneath was positioned in the right spot. I had to look as good as I could. He would need me to look presentable. Even if I was super uncomfortable, I knew Morgan would want me to dress up and be happy so I would be what he needed.

Shifting to the door, I stood holding the doorknob for a few moments. I had bought a house next to the church we were supposed to *get married in because it was a very lovely location. A few steps and I would be in the church.*

A knock on the door interrupted my thoughts, and I opened the door to see Jenny standing holding her hands to her side with a small frown resting on her lips, "Hey, Mattie. Are you ready to go? It's about to start." She held out her arm, and I wrapped mine around hers. I closed and locked the door, before walking down the pathway to the church.

Everyone seemed to be here today, and I couldn't even remember half of the names of the people standing there. I didn't know Morgan had so many family and friends. I guess he really was one of the most popular people I know. I saw my mother and father standing at the door, handing out pamphlets. I took a deep breath and walked up the stairs to them.

"Hey, Mom. Hey, Dad."

They both gave me a look, my mother reached out her hand and pressed it to the top of mine, "How are you doing, Baby?"

I just gave a quick shrug, because I didn't know exactly how I was supposed to feel right now. I didn't know what exactly everyone wanted me to do in this situation. Was I supposed to make them all feel better by putting on a smile? Was I supposed to break down and cry uncontrollably while everyone awkwardly tried to make me feel better?

The long walk to the pew really upset me because everyone was looking at me and giving me sad looks. What was this supposed to accomplish? Nothing was going to change, so why did everyone look like I just needed to wake up?

"We are gathered here on this day to celebrate the life of a young man, who passed away in his prime. Even though this young man passed away much sooner than the world would have liked, Morgan Winters felt things most people could only wish for in their entire lifetimes. I would now like to invite Mrs. Winters to the podium, where she would like to read a letter she had found written by Morgan himself before he passed away in the hospital."

The whole building was quiet, and I sat at the edge of my seat. He wrote a letter before he died? Who was it to? What did it say?

"My son made it quite clear he was in love, and with this letter, he let the world know exactly how he felt before he left us.

Dear Family, Friends, and Mattieboy,

I feel no pain right now. I'm looking out the window into the glaring sunset and wishing I could stay longer, but I know this isn't what my life is planned for. I just want everyone to know I love them, and I want Mattieboy to know I will always be here with him. Maybe my soul will transfer to another person, and he can fall in love with that person. I want everyone to know, with my last breath, I thought about how happy Mattieboy has made me, even if it was for a very short period of time."

She went quiet, bowing her head.

A few sobs rang throughout the building, and everyone seemed to be looking at me. I hated when everyone would stare at me. I took a deep breath, turning to Jenny, who at that point was holding back all her tears.

That's when I started crying. That's when I couldn't hold it back anymore. I had been trying to be strong for the last few days, and it all just came crashing down. Everything we had been through, everything we had done for each other had never been enough. He was going to leave me, and I could do nothing to stop it. I just let everything come out. I just let everything come to the surface, and I let it all out.

Jenny wrapped her arms around me as I cried, as I let everyone stare at the mess I had become. I didn't care. I just wanted Morgan to come back to me and love me like he said he would, forever and ever with no compromise. This was not part of my plan, none of this was.

What seemed like hours passed, and I just wanted to go home. Stepping outside the church, I was suddenly drenched as the rain was coming down in buckets. I guess it symbolized my feelings right now. I just started walking. I passed the house I bought and made my way to the cemetery, stopping at the freshly dug grave.

I ran my fingers over the letters and sighed.

"Morgan, how am I supposed to do this without you? How can I go on?"

Epilogue

I watched as the most beautiful woman I have ever seen walking down the stairs. Her vibrant blonde hair tied in a tight bun at the back of her head. The stunning white dress flowed down around her, making her feet look invisible in the white heeled shoes. Her face was made up to be more beautiful than I ever imagined, and her eyes were sparkling with the blue eye shadow that was placed above her already blue eyes. A smile was plastered on her face, and although I knew she was happy, she looked more nervous than I had ever seen her. I remembered her in high school as the loud and boisterous girl who would out-yell anyone she came across, but now I don't think she could even find her voice.

"You look... breathtaking." I quickly stood up from the seat I had been sitting in for the last half-hour, amusing myself with the game on my phones. I hadn't expected to see her like this so soon. I hadn't expected her to take my breath away so quickly. "He's the luckiest man alive.

Honestly, Jenny, you could make the Gods cry right now."

A quick slap to my arm and a few blushes later, she put her arm around mine and walked to the door, "I wouldn't want anyone else to walk with me down the aisle as much as I want you to right now, Mattie. You've been through everything with me. You've seen all my worst times and my best times. Thank you so much for coming with me."

I choked back a few tears, rolling my eyes slightly, "I'm not the only one that'll be walking you down this aisle, remember your father. He'll be right beside you the whole time, even if he's not physically there."

Carefully wiping her eyes, Jenny rolled up the front of her dress, "I know, but it's you who's going to get me to where I need to be. I lost two of the most important people in my life, and I am so glad that you're here with me. You're the brother I never had, but the brother I will always cherish. You make people happy by just being you, and I hope one day, I'll walk you down this aisle once and for all."

I had to chuckle at the last part, but before I could continue the conversation, the music outside the door started playing. Taking a few deep breaths, Jenny turned to me and half-smiled, "Am I doing the right thing?"

A quick slap to her arm and a few words later, I looked her in the eyes and smiled, "You're going to make the most beautiful wife ever known to man. Julian is so gosh darn lucky to have you. I can't wait until you start making babies, and I can give them lots of sugar and leave them with you."

She laughed lightly as the door opened, and people stood up and turned to see us walking. I felt myself turning red, not wanting all the attention to be around me. I just had to remember they were here for Jenny and Julian, and they were not staring at me. As we walked to the front of the aisle, I let her go with a slight peck to the cheek.

I don't remember much more about the ceremony. I just watched as they said their *I do's* and kissed in front of everyone. We retreated to the dinner hall, and sitting in front of everyone gave me the nervous shakes. Thankfully, Jenny made sure I was alright, and every so often her gentle hand would find my thigh with a gentle squeeze, assuring me everything would be okay.

Dinner and dancing commenced later on, and everyone was having a great time and seemed to be enjoying each other's presence. Standing in the back corner, I watched as everyone danced with their significant others, slightly making me jealous at the thought of not having anyone. In five years, I hadn't even thought of dating; I hadn't even wanted to think about finding someone else.

Sure, I went on dates and everything, but nobody ever fit the profile just right. I moved from the wall to retrieve another glass of punch from the bowl, and sipped on the red juice that somehow found its way down my chin. Grabbing a napkin, I quickly cleaned myself up. I watched Jenny laugh with her new husband, someone I would call a good friend.

"You seem to be having a terrible time. Are you lonely or something?"

I turned to see Mrs. Winters, a glass in her right hand, her left resting on one of the chairs nearby. "You don't seem to be enjoying yourself as much as you would like people to believe. How are you holding up? I know you would have loved Mr. Winters to be here right now."

She gave me a shallow smile, "We all don't get what we want, Mattie. You and I know that best out of everyone here, am I right?"

I gave her a slight chuckle, nothing too over-the-top, I knew exactly what she meant when she was talking about it. I wished for so long everything I did had included Morgan, but she was just as lonely as I was. A few months after Morgan passed away, Mr. Winters was in a plane crash, ending his life far too short as well.

"Shall we dance?"

Mrs. Winters giggled, "I suppose the mother of the bride and the pretty much brother of the bride should look a little more lively, shouldn't we?" She took my hand and walked on the dance floor, swaying with the slow songs that came out of the speakers.

I was in my own little world at that moment, just enjoying being with someone who understood. The music seemed to blend together until someone interrupted us. "I'm sorry, may I dance with this gorgeous man?"

I opened my eyes to see a man standing next to Mrs. Winters, "Oh, Mattie, this is Jenny's cousin, Myles Summers."

Bonus Halloween Chapter

It had always been my favourite time of the year, even in front of Christmas and New Year's. I loved dressing up in a silly costume and pretending I was young enough to trick-or-treat. This year would be different though. Morgan and I were taking his little cousin Kendall out, so we could get some free candy as well. I was at that age where I could just go to the store and buy my own supply of chocolate, but the free stuff always seemed to taste much better.

"Are you almost ready? We'll be leaving in a few minutes?" Morgan yelled up the stairs that I was taking my sweet time getting ready. I was Dracula this year, and if I knew anything, I had to look the part. People tended to give you more free stuff if you were dressed pretty much exactly like the character.

When I was seven, I was the guy from Zoolander, and someone ended up giving me twenty bucks because I looked so identical. When you're seven years old, twenty dollars is a hell of a lot of money. I ended up spending it all on candies at the corner store, and that's when I got my first cavity.

"I'll be done in a few minutes, you cannot rush perfection," I yelled back down. I was annoyed because he was in such a hurry, but I figured it wasn't Morgan who was getting impatient. I turned around to see a small child waiting by the door.

My breath got caught in my throat as I looked down at Kendall dressed in a small kitten outfit. I wanted to squeal like a girl in excitement, but I was able to keep it down, well... most of it.

"Kendall! You are adorable!"

Rolling his eyes, he trotted out of the room with his cute little tail swaying as he walked. It took me so much effort not to run over and squeeze the little cutie to death. I finished with my makeup and put it away. I grabbed my pillowcase and headed down the stairs. My cape flapped as I walked, which kind of made me excited this was happening. This year would be absolutely beautiful, even if some people thought I was too old for treats.

As I walked down the steps, I noticed Morgan was dressed as himself. I was slightly disappointed until I got closer and saw the tears of shredded cloth and blood dripping around his costume. I was slightly amused. He had dressed as a zombie. If he ever turned into one, I had to say he would make a pretty sexy zombie, I'd let him bite me.

"Well, don't you just look absolutely amusing. How long did that take you?"

Morgan gave me a smirk, "Not as long as it took you to put that makeup on. Are you ready to go? Kendall is about to pee his pants in excitement." He motioned his finger towards the small cat, and again I had to hold back the squeal. "He wants candy more than you want to look perfect, so we better go."

I gave Kendall a serious look, "Kendall, I just have one thing to ask you before we leave. This is very important. You cannot leave until I know you are ready!"

"Hold someone's hand when crossing the street, don't eat any candy until it's inspected, and always say thank you. I know the drill Uncle Mattie, I'm not two." He gave me the look, and I couldn't help but start laughing. It took a few seconds to regain my composure, but I went back to my serious look.

"No, that is not the question I have. I know you know those rules, but I need to know something else. If you answer wrong, we cannot go trick-or-treating."

Kendall's eyes got slightly bigger at the mention of not going, and he looked me up at me. Those cute little green eyes looked like he was about to start crying, "What? W-what do I need to know?" He was terrified he didn't know the answer, and we wouldn't be going. Morgan gave me a slight look, wondering what the hell I was up to.

I cleared my throat, "Give me your BEST cat impression!?"

Morgan started laughing, holding his stomach lightly as he watched Kendall, "You heard the man, what is your impression?"

Kendall looked at me, a small smile replacing the frown from earlier, and he meowed as loud as he could, making sure to growl at the end. I started laughing as well, impressed by the little kid. "Good job! You make sure you do that at every house, and we'll have so much candy you won't sleep for a week off the sugar!"

Giving me a satisfied look, Kendall opened the door and motioned for us to follow. I guess it was the start of the day. We all walked out of the house, locking the door behind us. As we walked down the street, I was impressed with all the costumes that we saw. I smiled as cute little kids walked around in their little costumes. I even saw a Thing 1 and Thing 2 twin costume on some babies.

We walked up to the first house, knocking on the door and backing up. A man opened the door and smiled, "Well, I see we have three people dressed to impress." He looked down at Kendall, "Your costume is the best I have seen all night! I love cats." He bent down to get ear level with Kendall, "I have five of my own."

Kendall clapped his hands with happiness, "I have two!" He looked around at what he could see of the house, before he noticed the cat sitting on the sofa, "I like that one! He's cute."

The man laughed as he got up and grabbed the bowl of candy from the table by the door, "You get an extra candy just for liking cats, but I think you get two more for having an awesome costume." He put the candy in Kendall's bag, and before we even had to say anything, Kendall thanked the man and turned around, ready to go to the next house.

We followed him from house to house, collecting candy from each person. A few people even gave us some candy, which excited me. I wouldn't have to go to the corner store and buy myself some sweets. As we finished the street, Kendall's bag started weighing down, so Morgan took it from him and slung it over his shoulders.

We started walking back to the house, and Kendall was yawning as we walked up the steps. His mother picked him up from the house a few hours later, and we decided to watch some scary movies. My head was resting on Morgan's legs as we watched Halloween. The night seemed to go on, and as I looked up at the clock for the final time, it was already three in the morning.

"I need sleep." I rolled off the couch, catching myself as I fell. Grabbing my phone from the coffee table I made my way up the stairs and crawled into bed. A few seconds later I felt someone lie down beside me and wrap their arms around me.

"Mattieboy, are you still awake?"

I mumbled a quick yes. I wouldn't be for long.

"Mattieboy, I really do love you."

Dedications

I have a lot of people to thank for this book being brought to you. These people honestly brought to life the spark inside me that made me want to write. Without the support of these people, I wouldn't be where I am right now. The first person I need to thank is my grandmother, whose support has never stopped and I don't think ever will. She pushes me to be who I am and what I want to be.

I need to thank my best friend and editor Eryn Summers for going above and beyond. You're in my heart, ES!

There has been many others that I need to thank, but then I'd have to have another book about them. Jaret, Jenny, Robyn, Chantal, Amanda, Ashley, Casey, Holly and so many others. Thank you for always being there when I needed someone to kick my butt into gear!

Word from the Author

I love to write, and I have been since I was thirteen. My characters are like friends to me, and sometimes I wish I could live with them in their world. I have written well over 400 short stories, countless pieces of poetry and other novels.

Personal Website: EliSummers.com

Thank you again for reading the hell out of this story! I hope you'll enjoy the rest of my works when they are published! I send you all my love.

Sincerely,

Eli Summers

Made in the USA
Columbia, SC
18 June 2017